ABI AND THE BOY WHO LIED

KELSIE STELTING

For anyone who's ever fought to be themselves.

For questions, address kelsie@kelsiestelting.com.

Editing by Tricia Harden of Emerald Eyes Editing

Cover design by Najla Qamber Designs

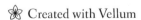 Created with Vellum

CHAPTER ONE

HOW JON MANAGED to look even better in a mortar board with a gold tassel hanging over his face, I didn't know. It wasn't fair.

He caught me staring and turned his smile on me. "What?"

Grandma yelled, "One more," twisting the dial on the back of the plastic camera to set it for another photo.

The first thing I was going to do once I had some extra spending money was buy Grandma a digital camera. This disposable camera business was getting old, and she refused to take photos on her phone. Her thumb always got in the way.

Jon shook my shoulder, grinning, and I rolled my

eyes up at him. I could only stay exasperated for so long when it came to Jon.

"Right there!" Grandma yelled, and the camera clicked with the shot.

I wished I could freeze this moment forever, staring into Jon's eyes, knowing that for whatever reason those eyes, that person, *saw* me. Broken pieces and all.

I read somewhere—probably in one of Grandma's magazines—that some cultures fixed broken vases with gold. The liquified metal filled each of the cracks and made a design even more beautiful than before. The flaw made it even better.

I hoped that was me. That somehow my past had weaved its way through my broken bits, and when I came back together, I was more interesting, more beautiful, worth more for all the struggles.

"I'm going to get your parents," Grandma said to Jon. "See you at graduation."

"Bye," I said, barely able to tear my gaze from Jon.

He tilted his head, still waiting for an answer as to why I'd been staring at him.

"How do you look so good?" I asked.

He chuckled low and brushed his nose against mine. "How do *you* look so good?"

I rolled my eyes again. He was delusional. But I wasn't complaining. I'd worked hard to fit into this dress—even if it was covered by a shapeless graduation gown.

"Abi," Grandma called from beside the mailbox. She held up a blue envelope. "Looks like someone got their card in the mail right on time."

I grinned. "I hope this one has money."

She brought it over to me. "If it does, chili's on you."

I shook my head. "We'll see. Meet you at the cook-off?"

"That's the plan," she said. "Should save us some time in all the commencement hubbub."

I smiled. "See you."

Jon and I walked together to his car and got in. As he pulled away from the house, I tore open the card. On the front, it said: Well wishes to the grad.

On the inside, written in block letters: *Enjoy it while you can.*

My chest constricted. What was this?

I flipped the card over, looking for a name, a signature, something that hinted this was a joke and not a threat, but there wasn't even a return address on the envelope.

"No money?" Jon asked.

I swallowed and shook my head.

"Guess your grandma's paying."

CHAPTER TWO

WHY WE DECIDED to have our graduation reception party at a chili cook-off two hours away, I didn't know. Well, I kind of did.

Skye and Andrew were weirdly competitive about chili recipes, and this was the first competition of the "season-ing." A chili pun, which, according to Andrew, was part of the fun.

So, while they rode with their parents to make sure the chili was ready, the rest of us crammed into Evan's brand-new-used SUV, a graduation gift from his parents. Jon and I sat in the two seats that folded up in the very back, our feet touching.

The parents were riding together, carpooling where they could, which left us alone with two hours to take in what had just happened. We'd graduated from high school. Received our diplomas. Closed a major chapter in our lives. Soon we'd be saying goodbye.

As I looked at the people in our car, Frank and Stormy pressed together in the middle seat, Evan and his girlfriend, Michele, arguing playfully over music in the front seat, Roberto staring out the window with his freshly buzzed hair, and Leanne and Macy quietly scrolling through Macy's phone, I couldn't help but feel like we were at a fork in the road. Destined to part ways. I just hoped the road would bring us back together somehow. That Jon and I could stay on the same path.

Jon laced his fingers through mine, and I squeezed his hand back. I'd never get tired of the way his touch sent warmth through my entire body.

"Why are Johnson and Scoller so far apart in the alphabet?" he asked. "I wished I could have sat by you."

My lips spread into a smile. "Why's that?"

He leaned closer and placed a slow kiss on my cheek. "So I could do that." Then he pressed his lips to mine. "And that."

My heart sped. "Yeah?"

It would have been nice to have Jon sitting by

me. I spent the entire ceremony trying to push the graduation card out of my mind.

"Seriously?" Roberto yelled. "I can't be surrounded by this."

Jon laughed against my lips and pulled away. I kept ahold of his hand, though.

Roberto shook his head. "You just want a nice trip with your *amigos*, and this is what you get." He pointed at each of us. "Couple. Couple. Couple. Couple." He pointed to himself. "Forever alone."

Frank broke apart from Stormy long enough to clap Roberto's shoulder. "You'll find a nice *chicka* someday."

Stormy laughed. "It's cheek-ah, not chick-ah."

Frank shrugged. "Close enough."

Michele eyed him. "I can't tell whether that's racist or not."

Frank pointed at her. "Juniors don't get a say."

She pretended to pout, but soon was smiling.

"Gosh, I love you guys." I said it out loud, even though I only meant to think it.

Jon squeezed my hand. How he managed to say so much with such a simple gesture, I'd never understand.

"Now," he said low, his green eyes gleaming. "Where did we leave off?"

CHAPTER THREE

EVAN DROVE along a dirt road by some fair-grounds. The frames of shut-down carnival rides looked more like a sad ghost town skeleton than the busy place it would be later this summer.

When he passed a white tin building, his GPS told him we had arrived, but we probably could have figured it out from the full dirt parking lot. There were vehicles everywhere, mostly trucks with mud spatters and guns hanging in the back glass.

"And I thought McClellan was redneck," I said.

Jon smirked. "I mean, it is."

I rolled my eyes. "There's redneck, and then there's 'grab yer guns, grab yer wife, git-r-done' redneck."

"Oh, I didn't know there was a distinction?"

I shoved him. "Get out, smart aleck."

"It's Jon, but okay."

I snorted. I loved this carefree, fun side of him. It seemed to be coming out more and more, the longer we were together. In a week, it would be two months. Two months of perfection I never thought I'd get.

I followed him out of the car, and we all walked inside together. Rows and rows of white folding tables covered in Crockpots lined the building. There had to be at least fifty competitors there, and they were all wearing team T-shirts.

"What is this place?" Stormy asked, giggling.

Evan grinned. "Chili." He laughed. "Like Chile. Get it?"

Macy shoved his shoulder playfully. "You needed Andrew to hear that if you wanted someone to laugh."

That made me smile. It was true. We each paid our way in and then started walking around. Our parents—my grandma—filed in a little later. I caught sight of Andrew's family, Skye's family, chatting with each other.

"Come on," I said to Jon. We walked, hand-in-hand, to their group. My eyes immediately took in Skye and her sister, wearing matching "Chili Beans" shirts. Her sister held a baby who couldn't have been more than a few months old in a "Chili Beans" onesie. The baby had these beautiful, wide blue eyes and dark hair.

"Oh my gosh, she's so precious," I gushed.

Skye's sister, Liz I think, grinned. "She takes after Dorian."

"Dorian?" I glanced around and... My mouth fell open. "Dorian *Gray?*"

This guy I'd only seen on social media or on music cover art on my phone grinned back at me, his eyes smoldering. My mouth fell open, then closed. Holy speechless fangirl.

Jon stuck out his hand. You know, like a normal human, and shook the *alternative rock star's* hand. "I'm Jon. This is my *girlfriend*, Abi."

The word girlfriend warmed me, snapped me back to reality. Yeah, maybe drooling over a famous guy in front of his fiancée/baby mama and my boyfriend wasn't a great idea. "Nice to meet you," I managed.

He smiled. "You too."

I was about to ask to hold the baby when Andrew came over and called us for a group meeting. "You can stay here, Skye. It's just grad reception, present stuff."

She shrugged and took the baby from her sister, holding her close to her chest. So sweet.

Andrew pulled us to a complete opposite corner of the building and handed each of us a giftbag. Stormy reached in to see what was inside, but Andrew yelled, "Wait!" He lowered his voice. "Wait. I want you to put these on right before the judging. And only right before the judging."

He hurried off, looking frazzled. Andrew never looked frazzled.

Our group stared at each other.

"Is he..." I asked.

Stormy pulled out the shirt, her mouth falling open, and nodded. "Looks like it."

CHAPTER FOUR

IF I FELT THIS NERVOUS, I didn't know how Andrew was still standing and walking around the chili cook-off. What would he do if Skye said no? Had he asked her parents already? What did Andrew's parents think of it?

But then I saw Skye and the way she was looking at Andrew, pure love in her eyes, and I knew none of that mattered. They belonged together.

I watched Jon where he stood several feet away, already talking to Grandma and his parents like life wouldn't permanently change for two of our closest friends after this day. We'd only been together two months, but if our relationship continued this way...would we be next?

I shook my head. Too soon. Too soon to think about things like this.

"Yo," Roberto said, coming to stand next to me. He pointed his spoon at his bowl. "You gotta try this menudo chili."

"Doesn't menudo have pig stomach in it?" I asked, eyeing the dish.

He held out a spoonful. "No."

I hesitantly took a sip, and flavors flooded my mouth, some savory, spicy, even a little sweet. "I know you're lying, but I don't care."

"I didn't lie," he responded. "It's cow stomach."

I closed my eyes, trying not to think about that.

He patted my back. "I'm gonna go before chunks fly."

"Good idea," I said, eyes still closed.

"Who was the card from?"

I opened one eye to see Grandma next to me.

My stomach twisted again, but not from the surprise ingredient. This time, it was fear.

"I don't know." I reached into my purse and showed her the letter.

Her lips pursed. "That's not a very funny prank."

"You think it was a prank?"

She rubbed my shoulder. "Of course. Kids are always getting up to stuff around graduation."

I nodded, remembering our class's senior prank. We took the Sinclair dinosaur from the shut-down gas station and put it on top of the school. How we managed to get away with that without getting caught...I didn't know.

Still, my stomach had an uneasy feeling as I tucked the card back inside my purse.

"How was the drive?" she asked.

My lips twitched as I thought of Jon looking at me, calling me beautiful, his fingers dancing along my skin. "It was good."

"Good." She held up a bowl of what looked like white chicken chili. "Have you found your favorite yet?"

I shrugged. I was trying not to eat too much for lunch since there was sure to be cake later. Plus, I had to do a five-mile run my college track coach had put on my summer workout plan. The idea of doing that with chili bouncing around my gut was a total appetite killer.

"This one might get my vote," she said.

"There's our grad," Marta announced, coming closer, Jon and Glen in tow. "We are so proud of you, honey." She wrapped me in a tight hug, the kind I wished my actual mom had given me, you know, before she got sentenced to prison time on drug and abuse charges.

I smiled into her shoulder. "Thank you."

"I need to get in on this," Glen said, and he wrapped his arms around the two of us.

I looked up and saw Jon smirking at me.

"I think Jon and Grandma better join in." I laughed and stuck my tongue out at him.

"Great idea," Grandma said.

We all held on to each other, and if I was being honest, it felt like having a family. This *was* my family, blood or not.

"I love you guys," I said.

The microphone squealed to life, making my ears burn. "Ouch."

We pulled apart, but Jon took my hand and said, "That's our cue."

CHAPTER FIVE

WE HURRIED to the one family bathroom in the building, but the door was already locked when we tried the handle.

"Occupied!" Stormy yelled.

Someone began speaking over the microphone about chili. How long would this go on before we needed to be back out there?

"Let us in," I said.

"Abi?"

"Yeah."

The door clicked open, and I saw six of my friends had filled the small space, in various stages of changing.

Leanne covered her chest with her T-shirt. "Shut the door."

We sidled in and locked the door behind us. I pulled my shirt out of the bag and laughed at the words on the front. *I love you from my head to-ma-toes.*

I couldn't get the giddy smile off my face as I pulled it over my head. "Ready?"

Everyone nodded or said variations of yes.

"Here's the plan," Evan said. "Andrew thinks his chili's going to win, and when it does, he's going to call us up to the stage—"

Andrew's voice came over the microphone. "Can my friends come to the stage?"

Evan's eyes glinted. "That's us. Let's get out there."

Jon slipped his fingers through mine. We held hands all the way to the stage, which was good, because mine were shaking.

I searched the crowd for Skye and easily found her right up front. She took in our shirts, and her eyes widened. Her lips formed Andrew's name in a question.

Andrew got off the stage and went to her. The crowd backed up and formed a halo around them. Silence filled the room.

"Skye," he said, "you are definitely the woman of my dreams and the most amazing person I could ever hope to spend the rest of my life with. And if you'll let me, I would love to make it official, because I already know I'm going to spend every day of the rest of my life with you—whether you like it or not." The crowd chuckled softly. "Please, make me the luckiest man alive and marry me."

Tears shined in her eyes as she dropped into his arms and cried, "Yes!"

* * *

That evening, all of us went to Denison Cemetery. But this time, we didn't streak. Freckles got some quilts from his trunk, and we spread them out. We lounged under the setting summer sun, drinking wine coolers, eating leftover cupcakes, and talking about forever like we weren't about to say goodbye.

But we were. Roberto was going away to basic training next week. Evan would spend the summer working for his aunt and uncle in Illinois. Andrew and Skye would spend as much of their summer together as they could before going to college on the east coast. Macy and Leanne had enrolled in a summer drama program at their college. Jon and I would leave for the track and field training camp in a couple of weeks. Stormy and Frankie were the only ones staying in town, working full-time.

I lay back on Jon's stomach with his arm draped over my shoulder and his hand resting on top of mine. I played with his fingers, calloused from weight training. I liked the way the little marks formed along the top of his palm and contrasted with the rest of his skin. Something about him had to be imperfect.

"I'm going to miss this," Stormy said. "Promise we'll do this again over Christmas break?"

"It might be a little cold," Andrew teased.

She threw a balled-up cupcake wrapper at him. "I mean us, hanging out together." Her eyes searched our group, a hint of desperation there. "You won't just leave us behind, will you?"

Frank squeezed her hand while Evan said, "We wouldn't dream of it."

A smile touched my lips. A world without my friends wouldn't be worth living in.

CHAPTER SIX

FEELING like we had a countdown clock over our heads wasn't fun. Part of me looked forward to college, but another part of me wanted to stay here forever. Moving was scary. I shuddered, remembering the drive to Woodman in a caseworker's car, everything I owned shoved into a black garbage bag. I didn't know it then, but now I had everything I needed in Woodman. There was my grandma, who loved me, the Scollers, who were like a second family, my best friends, and a great part-time job.

Still, there was a calendar hanging on my wall with daily workouts planned until we left for college. It stared back at me, an unplanned countdown to when my life would be uprooted yet again. We left in two weeks for a mandatory team training camp.

With Jon and me being distance runners, we'd mostly be doing a lot of conditioning. Like we were now.

I'd marked other dates on the calendar, though. My period, a dentist appointment, the day we'd drop Roberto off at the Austin airport for basic training, and the day Jon and I would pack up our stuff and leave Woodman behind.

A knock sounded on my door, and Jon poked his head in. "Ready to go?"

I cleared my expression and nodded. "Yeah. Let me grab my bag."

He walked out and called to my grandma, "Okay, I have time for a cookie!"

I rolled my eyes at his back but couldn't help smiling. Grandma always kept a junk food stockpile for Jon.

After picking up my purse, I stopped in front of the mirror and checked my reflection one more time. What did one wear on a date at a trampoline park? I'd opted for the leggings and shirt Jon's family had given me for Christmas. When I first tried them on, they'd been skintight, but now there was even a little gap between my midsection and the shirt.

My lips turned up at the image. This new training plan wasn't just getting me ready to be a collegiate athlete—it was transforming my body even more. I kept an old picture of myself on the mirror next to a recent one, just to remember what I used to look like. To see how far I'd come. I couldn't imagine ever going back.

Only forward. And now I was moving forward with Jon.

I left my room and found him sitting in the living room, eating a chocolate chip cookie the size of his head.

"Give me a piece," I said.

He broke off a little bit and handed it to me. I savored it as he stood up and thanked my grandma.

She smiled at the two of us. "Have I ever said 'I told you so'?"

"Yes," I replied. "Countless times."

She laughed. "Well, I'll say it again. Told you that you two would be going steady."

Jon took my head under his arm and rubbed it with his knuckles. "I'm not letting this one get away."

I shoved him off. "You're ridiculous."

"You're cute."

Grandma's lips went from a smile to a full-blown grin. "Okay, go on, go on. Have fun."

We walked down the sidewalk together, holding hands even though the Texas heat blazed down on us. My hand was already sweating. When we reached the car and I walked to my side, I tried to be surreptitious about wiping my palm on my pants. Sweaty hands—not sexy.

The trampoline park was in Austin, an hour away. I settled in for a longer drive, which meant I took hold of Jon's hand again and leaned back in my seat. I loved road trips now. It meant we had uninterrupted time to talk and just be...us. Our relationship was still so new, but it seemed right too.

Jon drove out of our neighborhood, telling me about the latest grueling workout on his list.

I definitely related. "It'll be a miracle if my legs don't fall off before we even get to Upton."

"Have you tried an ice bath?"

"You're kidding. I said I wanted to be out of pain, not subjected to more of it."

He laughed. "Really, it helps your muscles heal faster. It's good for you."

"Yeah right."

He lifted an eyebrow and gave me the smolder as he came to a stoplight. "What if we did it together?"

My stomach clenched. I knew he meant taking a bath, but... "Do it?"

Jon tossed his head back and laughed. "Only if you want to." He gave me a cheesy wink.

Okay, he was laughing, which meant it was a joke, but I was completely unprepared for that response. So I took a swig from my water bottle, nearly choked on the drink, and then ended up in a coughing fit, entirely derailing the conversation.

Smooth, Abi. Real smooth.

But even as my focus shifted away from my inability to swallow without risking asphyxiation, Jon's words still played in my mind. *Only if you want to.*

CHAPTER SEVEN

AS I LOOKED around the trampoline area full of children, I felt one thing: big.

They were all so tiny, and even though I'd lost weight, 5'10' was still tall. Especially for a girl. I wrapped my arms around my stomach and turned to Jon. "Are you sure about this?"

He easily took my hand and stepped onto a trampoline. "Come on; it's fun."

My arm bounced up and down with him, making it impossible not to giggle and jump on with him. Okay, maybe he was right. This was fun.

"Know any tricks?" I asked.

He scoffed. "'Know any tricks?' I invented tricks."

I laughed and raised my eyebrows at him. "Oh really?"

He nodded as well as a person could while bouncing on a springy surface. His jumps got higher and higher until he'd done a backflip and then a front flip. This kid from a couple trampolines over yelled, "Mom! Did you see that?"

"Show off," I laughed at Jon.

He slowed until he was just standing and then wrapped his arms around my waist and pulled me close. "I've gotta impress this girl I know."

"Oh yeah?" I asked, brushing my nose against his. "Who's that?"

"I could tell you, but it'd be easier if..." Slowly, he pressed his lips to mine, sending shockwaves through my entire body.

I lost myself to the kiss, until that same kid from earlier was screaming, "EWWWW!"

Jon laughed against my lips, and I swore it didn't get any better than this. How had I gone from the girl who barely fit on the seat next to him on the bus to the one who'd been dating him for two months? Who was kissing him now?

I didn't know. I just wanted it to last.

He wound his fingers through mine. "Come on," he breathed.

I would have followed him anywhere, even bouncing over the trampolines to the back of the building where hardly any children played. Going to the trampoline park on a weekday had been a good idea. We came to a huge mat that rose at least ten feet over a pit of foam blocks.

"Ready?" he asked.

Before I could think about it, I jumped. For a second, I felt weightless, free, terrified, but finally terrified of something other than not being good enough, of the strange note I'd gotten. I landed amongst the blocks and bounced once before sinking down, surrounded by softness.

Jon landed a couple feet away and started crawling toward me. We were buried low enough in the pit that the only way someone could see us would be from up above. This had been his idea all along.

Once he got closer, I picked up a cube and tossed it at him. It bounced off his head, and I let out a laugh. "Gotcha!"

"Oh really?" His smile turned mischievous, and he pounced on me, tickling me until I was gasping for air between breaths.

"Mercy!" I finally cried.

Laughing, he dropped back and propped himself

up beside me—as much as he could on such a soft surface. "Now that I've got you alone..." He waggled his eyebrows.

"There are too many children here for..." I waggled my eyebrows back.

"Well, fine." He pretended to dramatically fall back on the foam, dropping his hand across his forehead.

I lay beside him, laughing. "Can we just stay here forever?"

"I wish."

I was torn between wanting to stay in this moment and looking forward to our future. Even though college scared me, we would have our own spaces, our own rules, countless possibilities—both good and bad. What would it be like to visit Jon in his dorm room for the first time?

A new fear shot through my gut. What if he didn't want to visit me anymore, now that there would be countless girls to choose from, infinitely more gorgeous than me? Ones that carried less baggage?

"What are you thinking about?" he asked.

"Nothing." I bit my lip.

He reached over and brushed his thumb against my chin, freeing my lip, sending a trail of fire to blend with the uncertainty in my stomach. "What is it?"

I closed my eyes. I had to be honest, vulnerable. Something I wasn't good at in the slightest. So I kept my eyes closed as I said, "I'm worried about us."

I peeked one eye open to see his reaction.

A hurt expression laced his features. "You're not sure about us?"

That falling feeling was back in my core. The guilty one that knew I should be excited for this opportunity. For him and me. "I am. It's just... College will be different." I turned my eyes away from him. "What if you get to there and realize I'm not what you want?"

"Abi." His voice was firm but his touch soft as he cupped my cheek and turned my face to him. "I made the mistake of keeping my distance once. That's never going to happen again. I will be there for you, whether we're here or at Upton. Okay?"

The emotion in his eyes said he was telling the truth, but I still needed to ask, "Promise?"

"I promise," he said. And then he sealed it with a kiss.

CHAPTER EIGHT

WE STAYED in Austin after the trampoline park outing and spent our time walking around the mall, holding hands, trying to avoid the cookie dough shop. When we got home to Woodman, he stopped in front of Grandma's house to drop me off.

Even though the car was in park, neither of us moved. There, sitting so close to him, I never wanted to leave. I could have spent every day, every hour, having those green eyes and that smile all to myself.

"I love you," I said, unable to keep it all in.

"I love you more."

"I love you most."

He smiled a squinty-eyed smile at me. "I don't know about that."

"Tie?" I suggested.

"I don't know." He leaned across the console and kissed me. "When I'm with you, I always feel like I've won."

My cheeks heated, along with the rest of my body, regardless of how cheesy that comment was. If Old Abi could see me melting like this, she'd flick my ear and roll her eyes.

New Abi grinned at Jon and said, "See you after work tomorrow?"

"Of course."

I gave him a last smile as I got out of the car. Before going inside, I went to the mailbox to check the mail. By the time I closed the lid, he was already parked in his driveway.

He got out and yelled at me, "It's hard to say goodbye when you're this close!"

I laughed. "It's harder when you're far away."

"Good thing we're moving to the same town!"

I agreed. "Goodnight, Jon."

"Goodnight, beautiful," he called, loud enough for the entire neighborhood to hear, and I fell into another bout of disbelief. He hadn't shouted his love for me from the rooftops, but close enough. How had I gotten so lucky?

I smiled as he went inside, and began sifting through the letters from our mailbox. There were several bills for Grandma, a few college brochures—they were way behind the curve. Although, maybe I was too. I only signed at Upton University on a track scholarship a week before graduation. Hadn't applied anywhere else.

My heart and hand stalled on a letter addressed to me in the same block lettering as the graduation card. There was no return address, but the post office processing stamp read Austin, TX.

It was like all the warmth from Jon's words had been sucked from the air and replaced with a vacuum that stole my breath. My legs shook as I walked inside.

Grandma grinned at me from her chair and muted the news. Looked like a seal had escaped the zoo in Dallas. How, I had no clue.

"How was the date?" she asked.

"Good."

Her lips turned down. "You sure? You look like he fed you anchovies."

The thought was just weird enough to make me laugh. "No, it was fine." I reached out and handed her the mail, keeping mine to myself.

"I think I know what this is about," she said, eyeing the mail in my hand.

"Yeah, I—"

"I know it's hard to make a decision and feel like it's so final, but you should take the pressure off yourself," she continued. "A degree is a degree, and it doesn't matter where it comes from. Just what you do with it. And I know you're going to do great things."

I gave her a weak smile. "Thanks, Gram."

I couldn't ruin this moment, not right now. Especially since I didn't even know what the letter said. For all I knew, it could be the person admitting to the prank. I would be sure to tell them how *hilarious* it was. Ha. Ha.

The TV screen went black, and I saw Grandma setting the remote on her side table.

"I'm going to get some shut-eye, sweetie," she said and came to give me a hug. "I love you, and I am so proud of you."

I hugged her back, reminded of yet another thing I would miss when it came time to leave. "I love you, Grandma."

We said goodnight and went to our rooms. An ache settled in my chest as I sat on my bed and opened the plain white envelope. My mouth fell open at the line written inside.

CHAPTER NINE

Have a nice time in Austin?

I READ the line in block lettering over and over again, my stomach churning.

I thought about calling Jon, but I couldn't bring myself to pick up my phone and talk to him about it. That would make it too real. Give it to much credibility. Plus, something in me still held on to the hope that Grandma was right. That it was all a prank.

But we hadn't told any of our friends about the trampoline park date. At least I hadn't. Had Jon? But they would've had to sent the letter before we even went, or at least, the morning of. That didn't make any sense.

If I texted my friends and confronted them about

it, it would just lead to more questions. Questions I didn't want to answer. At least, not right now. Not with my heart racing like something bad was about to happen. I made sure my windows were locked with the curtains completely drawn and lay down in bed with the laptop I'd bought for college, thanks to the money I earned from my job with Mr. Scoller.

No amount of TV or books or blog posts or stupid cat videos on YouTube could get that line from the letter out of my mind. I just kept picturing the newspaper heading: *The Letter Killer. A B C You Later.*

Okay, it was a bad heading, but I couldn't come up with anything better when I was exhausted and it was 2 a.m.

Finally, I gave in and texted Jon.

Abi: Are you up?

Jon: No.

Abi: Seriously.

Jon: Are you okay?

What did I say to that? That I got a cryptic letter and now I couldn't sleep? I sighed and sent a text back.

Abi: I miss you.

Jon: I miss you too.

Abi: Can I ask you a favor?

Jon: Anything. Anytime. Always.

I didn't want to be that girl. The one who clung to her boyfriend so tightly the only thing he wanted to do was get away. But I couldn't get over this frozen, terrified feeling permeating my entire body.

Abi: Can we talk on the phone until I fall asleep?

Within seconds, my phone screen lit up with a call from Jon. I smiled at his picture, one of him from prom, looking stunning in his tux. I'd never seen someone clean up as well as he had.

I swiped the answer button and lay down with my cheek against the phone. "Hey," I said, sounding weaker than I wanted to.

"Hey, beautiful. Everything okay?"

"It is now."

He chuckled softly, but his tone was serious when he spoke. "You know, Abi, you don't have to be strong all the time. Sometimes our memories catch up with us, and we just have to wait them out. They're in our past, and we're always moving toward the future."

I agreed with him. But what if they weren't in the past? What if they were sitting on your nightstand, just waiting to make themselves a part of the present?

CHAPTER TEN

MY ALARM CLOCK WENT OFF, and I woke up with my face pressed against my phone, a little bit of drool dried on the black surface.

I groaned and pushed myself up, looking at the screen. One new text from Stormy. Before checking the message, I went back to my call log. Jon and I had stayed up for two hours and twenty-seven minutes, well past 4 a.m. I'd barely gotten two hours of sleep, and now I had to get dressed in business casual and go to work.

My feet sank into the carpet, and I stumbled to the bathroom, hoping a shower would wake me up. Plenty of hot water, two coffees, and four scrambled egg whites with dry wholegrain toast later, I was still dragging.

Mr. Scoller and the other partners had plenty of work for me, though. At least I wouldn't fall asleep on the job. Although, I was seriously considering researching horses to see how I could get some sleep standing up.

Around noon, my phone rang. Stormy.

"Hello?"

"Are you ignoring my texts?" she accused. I could hear all the sounds of the restaurant in the background.

"I'm so sorry." I rubbed my face. "I hardly got any sleep last night."

"Bow chicka wow wow."

"Ew, stop."

She laughed. "What? You've been together two months."

"Okay, new topic. What did you text about?"

"We're all going out to eat tonight, and then we're having a going-away party for Roberto at my place."

"I thought we were just doing breakfast with him tomorrow?"

"Girl," she said, "he's going to be in freaking humid, HOT North Carolina for ten weeks. No contact with the ladies, no beer, no nothing. We have to see him off the right way."

I laughed. "Okay. Where are we meeting?"

She named the restaurant and time, then said she had to get back to work. When I checked my text messages, I realized there'd been a whole thread in our group text, agreeing to go. Jon had even offered to pick me up.

Despite myself, I smiled. I liked that us going to a party together was the default now.

Just a little while longer until I could be with him. Feel his fingers slipping through mine, get some privacy for a kiss that would make me melt and freeze in all the right places.

I got back to work and threw myself into each task Mr. Scoller gave me, hoping for a distraction from the night before. Around five, Jon walked into the filing room where I was sorting papers. He wore shorts and a T-shirt, making them look like the clothes were designed specifically for him. If this moment were in the newspapers, it would say, *He's out of her league. Miracles do happen.*

And he looked like a miracle, even dressed so casually.

Mr. Scoller poked his head into the filing room. "Are you stealing my girl?"

"Sure am," Jon said. "But I think she's my girl, *Dad.*"

Glen winked. "That's my boy."

My cheeks heated. "Awkward."

They both laughed, and I stood up, storing the boxes I'd been working through so I could pick up where I left off the next day.

"Mr. Scoller, is it okay if I come in at noon tomorrow instead of eight?" I knew how Stormy's parties could go, and I didn't think I could take another night with only two hours of sleep.

"Sure thing," he said. "Just be sure to mark it on your time sheet."

"I will," I promised.

Jon took my hand, and we left the firm.

"We don't have to meet them for a couple hours," I said.

"You don't want to change?" His eyes trailed so slowly down and then up my body.

My stomach tightened.

"You're gonna make me look bad," he added.

"I hardly think that's possible."

"Whatever," I said. "Take me to Gram's, I'll change."

"Can I watch?"

I rolled my eyes at him and took his hand, not able to take the space between us any longer. "Let's go."

Jon kept his hand on my leg during the drive. Did he know how much his touch drove me crazy? That I couldn't focus on anything other than the spot of skin under his hand and the waves of attraction that radiated from that simple touch?

When he pulled his car into the driveway, I was both disappointed and relived. We walked inside the house together, and he followed me to my room. Grandma had left a note hanging on my door.

Went out to dinner with a friend. Be back around 8. Love, Gram.

Jon turned to me at the same time I turned to him. The look in his eyes told me he'd read the note and that he understood what it meant. We were at the house by ourselves, uninterrupted for at least two more hours, if we wanted to be late for our own dinner.

He didn't use words, just his touch, as he wrapped his arms around my waist and pulled me into a kiss that took my breath away. His lips lingered on mine, playing, tugging, savoring. My teeth caught his bottom lip, firm, for a fraction of a second, and a low moan escaped him from somewhere deep inside.

"Abi," he breathed, deepening the kiss. That one word did us both in as we walked to my bed, kissing, frantic, tasting everything we could in this PG-13 love scene I wanted to co-star in for my entire life.

Most of our time spent together was filled with talking or running or with friends and family, but this privacy, this *urgency* was new. And his hand, playing with the edge of my skirt, touching the bare skin of my back, my stomach, was new too.

I explored on my own, feeling his stomach, tight from track workouts, and the little bit of hair that grew on his chest, in contrast to his smooth skin of his shoulders. I couldn't breathe, didn't want to, because that meant another minute wasted, not kissing Jon, and I wanted to make the most of every second. This life seemed like a miracle to me. It could be any moment before he realized he could have some other —better—girl with him instead of me.

We kissed, explored, until my lips felt hot and my hair had come out of the carefully done braid I'd worn to work.

"We better get ready," Jon said against my lips.

"Do we have to?" I whined.

He laughed.

I was only partially kidding.

"Come on." He stood up and pulled me up off the bed.

As I went to my closet, all I could think was that I hoped my pillow still smelled like Jon when I went to bed that night, because I was going to be dreaming about this day for as long as I lived.

CHAPTER ELEVEN

WE SAT around the coffee table in Stormy's living room, and I just kept remembering that Saturday after my first track meet, playing Truth or Dare, laying my guts bare to these people who had gone from strangers to friends I couldn't picture my life without.

But this time, Jon sat beside me on a pillow. He kept brushing his shoulder against mine, sending an echo of the fire from earlier straight through my body. Whether he was doing it on purpose or not, I didn't know.

He caught me staring at him, smirked.

Definitely on purpose.

I shook my head at him, fighting a smile, and turned back to the conversation.

Andrew and Roberto were in a fire-round of Would You Rather, basic-training style, and all of our friends were cracking up.

Andrew stood toe-to-toe with him, yelling in his face like a drill sergeant. "Would you rather French your lieutenant or clean the dorms with a toothbrush?"

"How long was the French, sir?" Roberto fired back.

Andrew thought it over. "Two minutes, cadet."

"French," Roberto said. "Hands down. No homo." Then he gave an apologetic smile to Macy and Leanne. "No offense."

"None taken." Macy raised an eyebrow. "But you might not want to talk about hands down... you know, during a French with another guy."

Roberto's olive skin darkened red as he turned back to Andrew, stammering, "Next."

"Would you rather eat mud or throw it up, you worthless piece of pig bile?"

"Eat it," Roberto scoffed. "What kind of question is that?"

"Fine, would you rather get a sexy letter or a sexy picture?" Andrew asked.

"From you?" He laughed. "Neither."

Andrew pretended to be hurt, and Skye squeezed him tight. "It's okay, fiancé."

They'd been calling each other that all evening. It was one part cute, two parts gross.

I threw a pillow at them, laughing. "Get a room."

Andrew chucked it right back and went to stand. "Okay, where?"

Skye rolled her eyes, pulling him down.

He dropped beside her, easily slinging his arm around her shoulders, and dropped a kiss on her head. I'd been so jealous of their relationship only a few months ago, but now I felt like I had that, with Jon. Only, it wasn't so permanent. At least, not yet.

I shook my head to clear my thoughts. Why was I thinking about things like that? We hadn't even hit third base yet. Why was I thinking about forever?

Maybe that was the thing about forever. There was now, and then there was everything else. When you didn't have a good past, you just wanted to live in all the possibilities of the future. Of forever.

Andrew asked Roberto the next would you rather question, dropping the drill sergeant shout. "Would you rather stay in the U.S. or go overseas?"

It was the closest to real we'd been all evening, and everyone quieted, waiting for his answer. I could taste the tension in the room, feel it in the way Jon gripped my hand, more tightly than usual.

"Here," Roberto said. "I just needed a way out, you know?"

If anyone knew about needing a way out, it was me. I leaned forward and put a hand on his shoulder. "The fact that you said that means you're already halfway there."

His dark eyes met mine. "Thanks, *guera*."

Around four in the morning, after we'd talked and laughed and talked some more, someone decided we should get some sleep. Roberto had to leave at eight for the airport.

Jon curled up behind me on a bed made of couch cushions and blankets spread on the floor, and I leaned into his warmth. I fell asleep thinking about goodbyes and leaving and the letter and how sometimes, no matter how far away you wanted to get, your past could catch up with you.

CHAPTER TWELVE

EVAN WENT AROUND THE ROOM, waking us all up around six in the morning. We were taking Roberto to his favorite breakfast spot, which just happened to be the same place Jon took me to for breakfast the first time I stayed at Stormy's house.

None of us even bothered changing clothes. We just got out of our blanket nests and went to our cars, rubbing our eyes and yawning like the night owls we'd been.

Roberto rode in the Suburban with Evan and Michele. Even though they'd been together longer than Jon and I had, it seemed like they were where they should be three months in. Fun. Only a little gooey.

Jon and I, though... I couldn't take my eyes off his

jaw, where just the slightest amount of stubble grew. Where I would kiss him if we got another hour or two alone. It seemed like we'd skipped that early, testing-it-out stage altogether.

I cringed at the thought that we would both have roommates in college, a full course schedule, and track practices. That kind of time would be hard to come by, let alone privacy.

Jon parked right next to Andrew's car and came around to open the door for me. When we got inside, Skye, Stormy, and I went to the bathroom together. As we stared in the mirror, trying to make our faces look normal, Stormy said, "You and Jon looked cozy last night."

Skye waggled her eyebrows. "Sure did."

"Have you done it yet?" Stormy asked.

My cheeks heated as I shook my head.

Stormy's eyebrows came together, and she looked at me in the mirror like I was crazy. "Girl, what are you waiting for?"

Someone cleared their throat behind us, and a stall door opened. Marta came out, and my mouth went dry. If I'd been red before...

Marta put her hand on my shoulder. "They're waiting for marriage," she answered Stormy's question.

"Yep." I nodded. "That's it."

Marta gave me a knowing smile as she washed her hands. The second she walked out of the bathroom, I sagged down against the wall while Skye and Stormy burst out laughing.

"Shut up," I whisper-yelled. "The bathroom's not soundproof!"

Still, their shoulders shook from the force of their quieted laughter.

"Ha ha," I said. "Hilarious."

Stormy put her mascara back in her purse, then offered me her hands to help me up. "Sounds like you'll be waiting a while."

We left the bathroom to see Marta and Grandma standing by our table, talking to all of our friends. To Jon. I hadn't thought it possible, but my face got even redder than it had before. My neck and ears felt warm now too.

Marta smiled warmly at me. "I was just telling Jon how I ran into you in the bathroom."

Stormy sniggered behind me, and I elbowed her.

"My boob," she grunted quietly.

Humor sparked in Marta's eyes, which looked so much like Jon's. "I didn't know the going-away breakfast was here."

"That's my fault." Roberto held his hands up.

"This is my favorite. I had to get one last good meal in before I suffer through MREs for ten weeks."

Grandma smiled at him. "Don't you think for a second that we don't appreciate all you're doing, serving our country."

Roberto looked almost...bashful as he smiled at her and mumbled something about it being no problem.

"Well," Marta said. "We'll leave you kids to it. Hope you don't have to wait too long." She winked at me. "For your food."

The second the door closed behind them, Stormy and Skye broke out in laughter so hard I had to relate the entire painstakingly embarrassing encounter to the rest of our friends. If we were playing a game of Would You Rather, I would have rather had Marta walk into the bathroom on me naked than overhear that conversation.

Jon seemed amused by it all. "Mom was just joking. She knows that's not realistic."

His words made my back straighten and sent butterflies whirring in my stomach. Not realistic?

I didn't even know how that made me feel. How it *should* make me feel.

But there were bigger things to worry about, like

this being the last supper...breakfast, with all my friends in one place.

Everything was changing, and I felt the gold plating in my cracks shifting loose. I'd been through worse. So why did this feel so bad? Like losing a part of myself?

When eight o'clock came, Roberto's parents parked outside the restaurant in their vehicle that had already been packed with his bags.

They waited in the car while the ten of us stood in the parking lot, one big, awkward, teary crowd, none of us wanting to say goodbye first.

"Roberto," Stormy said, her eyes misty.

"Stop," he said, shifting. "I'm going to be gone for ten weeks. That's it."

"Yeah, but then..." Macy trailed off, her eyes taking on the same haze as Stormy's.

I could already feel the hole forming in my chest. Tears stung my eyes. We were a group. If anything, we were supposed to gain more friends. Not less.

Andrew let go of Skye's hand to give Roberto a hug. A real one. Not the stupid half one guys usually do. And then Evan did. And Stormy did, and we were all reaching to give him a hug goodbye.

As he squeezed his arms around me, he said, "We got out. We made it."

But this didn't feel like making it; it felt like losing it. "Be safe," I choked out.

We watched, a sad, rag-tag group minus one friend as Roberto's parents drove him away. He waved out of the backseat window, and we stayed, waving back until the car had driven so far away we couldn't see even a hint of it anymore.

CHAPTER THIRTEEN

EVAN LEFT TOWN next after another goodbye breakfast at the diner. A week after that, Andrew and Skye drove off in Andrew's Taurus, packed so full we couldn't see inside through the back windows. Skye held a lamp in her lap, and the back end sunk so low, I worried about their tires. Another week later, Macy and Leanne left right after breakfast, riding away with stuff piled high in the bed of Macy's dad's pickup.

And then it was my turn, Jon's turn, our turn.

While I finished packing my things into suitcases and storage tubs—I couldn't stand the sight of another black garbage bag—Stormy lay on my bed, throwing a round lip balm pod to the ceiling and catching it in a lazy rhythm. Up, down. Up, down.

"I still don't understand why you're just now packing," she said.

Because I don't want to leave. "I've been busy."

She caught the lip balm and sat up on the bed, applying it to her lips. "Busy doing nothing until marriage?"

My cheeks warmed. "Maybe." That was true enough. When I wasn't working, I was spending time with Jon or my friends, soaking up every minute I had before everything changed. Now change was unavoidable.

I turned my back to her and started on my dresser. The last part of my life in Woodman to get tucked away and transplanted to my dorm room. All my feelings from my last move bubbled up, but I had to remind myself this was different. My possessions were being stored in clean containers, not hastily shoved into garbage bags. I wasn't healing from bruises. I would be able to show my face, my strong new body, instead of hiding behind layers of make-up and baggy clothing. There would always be a place for me to come home to. Grandma had assured me of that.

"You sure you don't want help?" Stormy asked.

I shook my head, knowing she was watching me, and started transferring clothes into Grandma's suitcase. It was covered in cream and red roses, faded from years of use.

As I pulled a pair of jeans from the bottom drawer, two letters fell from inside the fold. Both with the same blocky handwriting.

I hastily shoved the notes in my bag, glancing over my shoulder to make sure Stormy hadn't seen.

She had.

She quirked a brow. "Love letters?"

I rolled my eyes, trying not to show how shaken up just holding them made me. "Something like that."

My heart pounding, I stood with the suitcase. The letters made it feel a thousand pounds heavier than it was.

No one had admitted to sending them, but they had stalled for the last few weeks. I hoped it meant they were done—not-so-funny game over.

"Need help loading it up?" Stormy asked.

I nodded. "Don't let Grandma see—"

"See what?" Grandma asked, coming in my room and gazing around. "You're not trying to keep me from helping, are you?"

"Nooo," I said sarcastically, handing her the smallest bag in my room. "Here, take this."

Grandma glared at me, an echo of my mom's

deadly stares, and she picked up a heavier box. "Good lord," she said, carrying them toward the front door. "I'm old, not an invalid."

Stormy and I exchanged glances. I cringed, but she grinned.

"Your grandma is goals," she said.

I couldn't disagree.

Stormy walked around to the back of my car. "How do you open this thing?"

I laughed. "The trunk's up here," I said, going to the front.

She shook her head. "I'll never get used to that."

The three of us made quick work of loading up my things, which all fit comfortably in the car, either in the trunk or back seat. I'd come with barely anything, and even though I was leaving with a lot more, I still didn't have much.

I shut the trunk and locked the doors. Grandma stood with her hands on her hips while Stormy and I sprawled out on the grass, breathing hard.

Stormy rolled her head toward me. "Why didn't Jon do this?"

"Because," Grandma said, "we are strong, capable women." She paused. "Well, you two are. I'm a helpless old lady, right, Abi?"

I pointed my gaze back at her, at the pleased

smile on her face, and started laughing. "Fine, Gram, you win."

She looked pleased. "Now, get inside and freshen up. We're going to be late."

CHAPTER FOURTEEN

WHY WE KEPT SAYING goodbye in public places, I didn't know. The entire time we ate lunch with Jon's family, Grandma, Frank, and Stormy, I felt seconds away from tearing up. Each swallow of my food had to go over this massive lump in my throat.

Yeah, Jon and I would be together, but what about Grandma? The woman who was there in the living room *every morning* when I woke up for my run, who offered me green tea and egg white omelets when I got back? Or Marta, who treated every Wednesday evening like a huge event with a three-course meal and cross-stitched place mats?

Or Stormy. Who'd somehow gone from a ray of hope to my enemy to the best friend I'd ever had.

What would life be like without them?

What would *I* be like without them?

After eating, we went out to the parking lot, walking slower than needed, even though it had to be more than a hundred degrees outside and some A/C would feel like heaven.

Marta squinted at me, her hand shading her eyes. "So, this is goodbye?"

I swallowed, nodded.

Without warning, she pulled me into a hug. "I know you have your grandma, but ever since that first night you ate at our house, I've thought of you as a daughter." She rubbed my back and pulled away. "You'll let me know if you need anything at all, right?"

I nodded. If this was how I handled my first goodbye, I was toast... full-blown, buttery, blubbery toast.

Glen squeezed me next while Grandma and Jon said their goodbyes. "We're going to miss you. At our house and at the firm."

I hugged him back. Marta said she thought of me as a daughter, but after months of seeing Mr. Scoller almost every day and working with him, I thought of him like a father. If Jon wasn't his son and it wouldn't be gross, I would have wished for him to be my dad.

"Take care," he said.

"You too." And I meant it. I couldn't imagine his life outside of being Jon's dad. This change would be hard for him too.

Then Grandma stood in front of me, and... I turned into a puddle right there, ready to evaporate under the late summer sun. She took me into her arms, holding me up. This woman had gone from being my grandma who lived a couple towns over to being my rock. She'd believed in me when society—my parents even—said I'd never amount to anything. She'd taken the shell of Abi and brought her back to life.

"Grandma," I began, but choked over the words I wanted to say. About how much I loved her and how I would miss seeing her in the evenings or being jealous about how she could out power-walk me, even at seventy years old. Instead, I sobbed into her shoulder. I'd been preparing for this day, this moment, but nothing could prepare me for this feeling of complete loss.

"Shh, shh," she soothed me, rocking me. "You listen to me," she said, a barely detectible waver in her voice. "You are amazing. You overcome obstacles, you love with your whole heart, and you *never* let what anyone thinks of you crowd out what you think of yourself. And when you start doubting yourself, you just come right back to me, and I'll tell you how much I love you. How much you should love yourself. You hear me?"

I nodded against her shoulder and managed the only words that mattered. "I love you too."

Her hand rubbed my arm, and she backed away until it fell at her side. "You're going to do great things. Just you wait and see." She squeezed my cheek.

"Ready to go?" Glen asked. "Give these kids some time to say goodbye?"

She nodded, reaching into her purse. In her grasp was a manila envelope. "I got your mail before we came here. You let me know your forwarding address so I can—"

"Get my mail forwarding set up," I finished. She'd already mentioned it a few times in the last couple days. "I will. I promise."

The business of it all held me together, at least while she, Glen, and Marta got into the Scollers' car, leaving the four of us friends to say our goodbyes. But without her, I was already wrecked.

"Abi..." Stormy began, but I shook my head, stuffing the envelope in my own purse.

"I can't take anymore," I said.

She took my shoulders and shook them. "What

are you talking about? You're Abi freaking Johnson. You can do anything."

I wiped at my nose. "That's not my middle name."

She snorted. "Jon, talk some sense into her."

He took my hand, squeezed, but he didn't try to talk me out of the pain. Instead, he said, "It's hard to say goodbye."

Stormy's lips faltered. "We're not saying goodbye."

"What do you call it?" I asked.

But Frank spoke first. "Go do something with your lives. We'll be here cheering you on."

I was pretty sure that was the most Frank had ever said at one time, but Stormy nodded like he'd captured it perfectly. Still, red rimmed her eyes, and she said with a false levity, "Just don't forget us little people, yeah, *chica*?"

Wearing a bittersweet smile, I shook my head and hugged her. "I could never. I love you, *chica*."

She smiled and pulled back. "Get out of here. It's time to chase your dreams."

CHAPTER FIFTEEN

WHEN I MOVED into Grandma's house, a case-worker—I didn't even remember his name—drove me the hour from McClellan to Woodman and dropped me off at her front door. I sat in the back seat of the white van, even though he'd offered to let me sit up front. I ate the fast food meal he'd gotten me, not really tasting it, just knowing I needed the reliability of food's comfort when everything in my life had been turned upside down.

How was I supposed to know what Woodman would hold for me? Friends, a family, a life?

Now, as I drove away from Woodman, tears streamed down my cheeks. A lunch box with healthy snacks sat in the passenger seat, even though Upton U was only a couple hours away.

Jon's car blurred in front of me, and I blinked away the tears, my eyelids clearing my eyes like windshield wipers.

My phone rang, and I reached out to answer it. Jon.

"Hello?"

"You know what I think?"

I sniffed. "That phone greetings are dumb?"

He laughed. "No. I think that this is going to be the best thing that ever happened to us."

"Yeah? Why?" I swiped at the tears on my cheeks. This didn't feel like the best thing.

"We're going to a great college, meeting all new people, getting the best in training advice, majoring in what we want...We're finally going to live life on our own terms. No ex-girlfriends or boyfriends, no parents, no friends. Just us against the world."

The corners of my lips twitched up. "Say that. Again."

"What? That we get to live life on our own terms?"

"No, the last part."

"It's just us against the world?"

"Mhmm," I said, setting my cruise. "Do you mean it?"

"I do," he replied. "Abi, there's no one else I want to have all these firsts with."

My stomach clenched, dropped, soared. All of my firsts would be with Jon. And I hoped my lasts would be too.

"How does that sound?" he asked.

"Like perfection."

I could practically hear his smile through the phone. "It does to me too."

We talked for the rest of the trip, sharing our hopes, dreams, fears, everything and nothing at all, growing closer even as we drove in separate vehicles toward an unknown future.

I wanted to believe in all these things, but as we pulled into a gas station on the outskirts of Austin and I waited for him to run in and use the bathroom, I realized how afraid I was to hope. Hoping and being disappointed was crushing. Fearing and being right was affirming, if nothing else.

I sighed and pull out the manila envelope Grandma gave me earlier. Might as well get rid of some junk mail before having to clean it all out of my dorm.

I flipped each of the envelopes forward on the stack and then froze. A single, white envelope with no return address and my name written in little block letters. My fingers trembled as I ripped open the back flap and saw the writing insde.

CHAPTER SIXTEEN

You won't last six months.

I WANTED to ball it up, throw it in the trash outside my window and never see this person's words again, but my fingers stayed frozen on the page. Was the letter a doubt in my abilities...or a threat?

When I glanced up, I saw Jon walking toward my car, and I hurried to shove the letter back in the manila envelope. I didn't know why I hid it from him. Telling him just didn't seem right, like it didn't fit in my relationship with Jon and this perfect dream he had for us. Stress, panic, over something I wasn't even sure amounted to more than a mean prank, wasn't worth worrying him.

He opened my door and handed me a Nerds rope.

I eyed it, already guessing how many calories it had and how hard I would need to work out to make up for the extra sugar intake.

"Live a little," Jon said, like he was reading my mind.

I looked up at him, unable to come up with a witty response or even a smile.

His eyes immediately shifted from brilliant to worried, and he squatted next to my car so we were closer to eye level. "What's going on?"

Um, maybe I'm moving away from the only real home I'd ever known to a place where, like the card suggested, I didn't even know if I'd make it through the first semester, let alone all four years. And I was on my own, other than a boyfriend who was likely less than a few months away from realizing how much better he could do than me. And I had a letter in my passenger seat, saying all of that in a single sentence.

But I didn't tell him that. I just shook my head, trying to swallow down the fire ball of a lump in my throat.

His palms covered my knees, and I tried to focus

my every thought on the warmth that lived there, but it was hard.

"Abi," he said, squeezing a little. "Look at me. Let me see those beautiful eyes."

My lashes fluttered, and I turned my eyes away for a moment, fighting tears. His thumb brushed under my chin, lifting my gaze.

"Hey," he breathed. "Are you scared?"

I nodded, letting him assume about what.

"I'm scared too."

Jon Scoller, afraid? He'd have everyone on campus in love with him within a matter of minutes. "What do you have to be afraid of?"

He smirked. "Maybe some jock stealing my girl."

I rolled my eyes and stole a line from *Clueless*. "As if."

"Maybe I'm not cut out for college courses. It's not like I was ever amazing at school."

"At least you didn't need a teacher to hand-feed you answers twice a week." I tried to keep the pain out of my voice at the mention of Mr. Pelosi. He'd been my saving grace that first semester at Woodman. Now I'd probably never see him again.

With an exasperated expression, he shook his head. "What if I can't juggle it all? College and track will be a lot."

The real fear behind his words showed through in the tightness of his eyes. And it struck me. Jon really was afraid. It wasn't right. His perfect features shouldn't be pinched like they were now.

I took his face in both of my hands and put my forehead to his, breathing for a moment. I hoped he could feel the love I had for him through the connection. "You're going to be amazing. You already are."

One of his hands covered mine on his cheek, and he pulled it away. The only thing that gave me any hope was the fact that he kept holding it, albeit loosely. He refused to meet my eyes as he said the next part. "You know I don't have any friends, right?"

My brows came together. "What do you mean? We hang out with my friends all the time."

"Right," he said. "*Your* friends. I can't think of a single person from Woodman, outside of my family, you, and your friends, that I want to stay in touch with. Don't you think there's something wrong with that?"

I chewed on my lip. "I'm the least qualified person to comment on that."

He groaned and buried his head in my shoulder. "What if there's something wrong with me?"

The very idea of him thinking there was anything wrong with him was like someone saying the sun was cold. It just didn't make sense. "Jon, I was being serious when I said you're amazing. There's not a doubt in my mind you'll fit right in."

His eyes seemed troubled, free of his usual confidence. "Promise you'll stay by my side, through it all?"

"Of course." I couldn't imagine it any other way.

CHAPTER SEVENTEEN

THE FARTHER we got into Austin, the more cars crowded the road, the harder it was to stick right behind Jon's car. Soon, traffic separated us, and his number flashed across my screen.

"I lost you," he said.

"I know," I grunted, holding the cell between my cheek and my shoulder. Driving a stick in the city called for two hands.

"Need me to pull over?"

"We're on the interstate," I argued. "You go ahead. I'll stop and plug it in my phone. Just...save me a spot, okay?"

"Promise."

I took the next exit and typed in the address. Even though I knew Jon would be waiting for me, I felt so much more alone. Energy thrummed through my body as I entered the freeway again, attempting to keep up with it all.

Eventually, finally, I saw the signs for freshman move-in. They unsettled me more.

Since Jon and I both went potluck on the roommate situation, I'd be meeting the person I'd live with for the next year in only moments. I hoped she wasn't weird or cult-y or any of the other horrifying ways movies portrayed terrible roommates.

But maybe if she was bad, that would give me just another reason to go see Jon in his dorm room...

I hit my signal and turned into the drive along the dorm building. The car in front of me slammed on its brakes, and I did too, effectively killing my engine. I glared at the guy who jumped out, and he gave me an apologetic look under dark wavy hair as his ride drove away.

"Sorry," he mouthed, his wide eyes earnest.

I looked away, trying to hide how embarrassed I was as I started my car back up. Finally, finally, finally, I was able to pull up behind Jon's car, where he stood with his arms folded over his chest, waiting.

He smiled at me through my windshield, and I smiled anxiously back at him, parked my car. I took a deep breath to still my shaking hands. This was it.

Jon opened the door for me and took my hand to pull me out. His gaze went to the campus around us. The tall brick building with rows and rows of windows where we'd be living—me on an even floor and him on an odd one.

"Home sweet home," he said.

This building would never be home, but standing next to Jon, tucked underneath his arm, I realized I had a piece of *home* with me.

I leaned my head against his shoulder, taking it all in, and he kissed the top of my head. "Everything's going to change," he said.

A girl who only looked a year or two older than us approached, wearing a blue polo with the Upton mascot—the *vaquero,* cowboy—right above her big breasts. Like, massive. How was she standing up? "Are you in the A building?" she asked.

I followed Jon's eyes, hoping they were going the right direction, and grinned when I saw he smiled at her face. "We are."

She took us to the big stand where they were checking people in, and part of me cringed at the fact that I was checking into my dorm at what equated to a lemonade stand. Like, *Welcome to college, that will be $50,000.* But I kept it to myself. With some effort.

Jon and I got our room keys. I would be on the

tenth floor, since freshmen had to room higher up, and he'd be on the ninth. It wasn't right next door, but pretty close.

We held up our keys and snapped a selfie to send to his parents and Grandma. After we pocketed our phones, we grabbed a cart and got started.

"We'll get your stuff in first," he said.

"We can do yours first," I offered.

His eyes narrowed. "You're putting off meeting your roommate, aren't you?"

I stood up on my tiptoes and kissed his cheek, nibbled on his earlobe.

"So that's a yes?" he mumbled. "I don't even care."

Someone a few feet off yelled at us to get a room.

Jon whispered against my lips, "What does it look like we're doing?"

I smiled and pulled back. "So, you first?"

A chuckle started low in his throat and spilled over his lips. "Nope." His eyes had lost that hazy look that came whenever our bodies talked instead of our words. He took hold of the cart and wheeled it toward the front of my car. "You can do this. She will love you, and you'll love her, and it will be great. Maybe she'll even be the maid of honor at our wedding."

I stood frozen. "Did you just say..."

At first, he looked confused. Then under-standing crossed his expression, then bashfulness. "Too soon?"

Smiling, I shook my head. Especially since I'd been thinking those thoughts all summer.

We made quick work of unloading my things, stacking them all up in one pile. Jon walked on one side, me on the other to make sure the suitcase tower didn't topple, and started our march inside. My throat got tighter the closer we got to room 1009. To whatever or whoever waited behind the door.

"You go in first," I whispered. "Make sure she hasn't painted the walls black or anything."

He gave me an exasperated smile but obliged, pushing the door open. "Hey," he said. "You look familiar."

CHAPTER EIGHTEEN

A VOICE CAME BACK, kind and clear. "You're Jon Scoller, right? From Woodman? I went to Roderdale."

Curiosity got the best of me, and I followed him into the room. A girl with bright blue eyes and brown hair knotted on top of her head stood on one side of the room, boxes stacked around her. Good thing I didn't have much, because I wasn't sure how our stuff and both of us were supposed to fit in the small room.

"Are you my roommate?" she asked, a nervous edge to her voice.

The fact that maybe she was as scared as I was immediately set me at ease. "I guess so. I'm Abi."

"Anika."

An awkward silence hung between us. What now?

"Why don't you guys get to know each other?" Jon suggested. "I'll go park your car?"

"Are you sure?" I asked. "I can come help."

"Yep." He stuck his hands out for my keys, and in moments, it was me, Anika, and a twelve by twelve room with cinderblock walls—painted white.

"I wanted to wait for you before picking a side." She gestured between the two loft beds. "Do you have a preference?"

Honestly, each side was a mirror of the other. I shook my head.

"Me either."

I dropped my backpack on the bed farthest from the door and unzipped it. So maybe the notes had me on edge. As I took out my school supplies and put them on the generic desk under my bed, I searched my mind for something—anything to say to Anika. There had to be something.

"Was that your boyfriend?" she asked. "He's cute."

I turned to gauge her expression. It seemed neutral, but maybe there was something hiding underneath? Maybe she liked him. Who wouldn't like Jon? "Yeah, he is. Are you dating anyone?" Please say yes.

"Yeah, Kyle Rayford," she answered. Her smile said she was happy about it, but there was a bitter sweetness in the tightness of her eyes that made me wonder if there was a story there. "Do you know him?"

My mind jumped back to the first football game I watched and how Stormy thought Kyle had a great backside. "Um, I've heard of him."

She climbed onto her bed, even though it didn't have any sheets on it and was probably covered with other people's germs and... I shuddered. Something that rhymed with germs. Gross.

I wanted to say something, but awkward Abi from a year ago took over. My throat felt dry, and all I wanted was a chocolate-coated granola bar and a sugary soda to give me a feel-good sugar boost. Instead, I got busy unpacking my suitcases and totes, trying not to think about food or if Anika was watching me or if she would like me or if this would be the most awkward year of my life. And that was saying something. I'd had a lot of awkward years. I used to have Bieber Fever, for crying out loud.

I was up on my bunk, trying to put on a fitted

sheet without breaking my neck, when Anika spoke next.

"Oh my gosh," she said. "We match."

"Huh?" It didn't look like we were wearing the same clothes.

She dug through one of her suitcases and pulled out the exact same sheets I had on my bed.

I laughed. "I guess you have good taste?"

"Or I saw the same sale at Target you did." She giggled.

"Accurate." In a final ugly grunt, I got the last corner of the sheet over my mattress and climbed down the ladder. Then I threw my flat sheet and comforter over the bunk and stood back to take it in. Anika's side of the room, still in boxes, and my side, an echo of the room I had at Grandma's.

"What are you doing tonight?" she asked.

I shrugged. "Jon and I hadn't talked about it."

"Want to go to the freshmen pancake feed?"

"Are they trying to fatten us up for slaughter?"

She laughed. "You're funny."

My cheeks warmed, and I mumbled a thanks.

"I think it's just to introduce us to people." She shrugged.

Jon walked in at that moment. "You're not gonna believe this."

Then, the second most handsome guy I'd seen in my life followed him into the room and announced, "We're roommates too."

Anika's face split into a grin as she sat up. "No way."

Jon nodded.

"That's amazing," I said.

Jon winked at me. "Looks like it will be easy to get some privacy."

Curse my damn pale skin for showing just how much the idea of privacy with Jon got to me. This was college. No rules.

The handsome guy, who had to be Anika's boyfriend, went and leaned against Anika's lofted bed, arms folded across his muscular chest.

I finally gathered myself enough to speak. "How did that even happen? This is too weird."

Kyle shrugged. "Apparently, they try to put athletes together. If they can."

I turned to Anika. "Are you out for track?"

She shook her head. "You must be leftovers."

I shrugged. I had signed up for the team late in the season.

Jon wrapped his arms around me. "Never." He dropped a kiss on top of my head, and I closed my eyes against his touch. I loved it. Loved him.

"So, what are y'all doing tonight?" Kyle asked.

Jon looked at me. "I'm taking my girl out."

The words just fell off his lips, but they torpedoed my heart. *His girl.* I liked the sound of that.

"Starting when?" I asked.

He took my hand. "Now."

CHAPTER NINETEEN

WE WALKED TOGETHER to his car, which was parked so far away, we practically needed a map and some snacks to get there.

He grabbed the handle with one hand and bent over with his other hand on his knee. "It was a tough run, but I'd like to thank my mom and dad for always supporting me, my girlfriend for letting me walk behind her from time to time, and my Lord and—"

"Unlock the door, Jon!" I laughed.

Chuckling, he hit the button and we climbed inside. As he pulled away from the college, I asked, "So, what are we doing?"

He smiled over at me. "Up for a little adventure?"

I would be up for anything with him. He could

suggest a marathon over a bed of hot coals, and I'd run it twice if it meant more time with him. But I just said, "Sure. Anywhere's good with me."

My phone dinged with a notification.

Grandma: Do you know your new address yet?

I sent it to her with my room number, and then I copied and pasted it into the friends group text.

Abi: In case one of you is nice enough to send a package. Or magical pants that can fit both Evan's skinny ass and mine. Whatever works.

Stormy: Laughing Emoji. You're more likely to get the pants.

Abi: Ouch.

Andrew: What about us? They don't even have Dairy Queen here.

Evan: Crying emoji. Baby emoji.

Andrew: Heyyyy.

"My phone's blowing up," Jon said. He took it out of his pocket and gave it a quick glance. "Group text?"

I tilted my head and gave him a smile. "What else?"

His hand settled on my thigh, rubbing up and down, sending sparks to my core.

Frank: Can we go back to the part about Abi getting in Freckles's pants? Smug face emoji.

Macy: I don't think Jon would like that.

Michele: Side-eye emoji.

Macy: Or junior over there.

Abi: Blushing emoji. Just kidding. Gah.

Frank: Uh huh. Winking emoji.

Abi: Eye roll emoji.

Abi: Going on a date with my ACTUAL boyfriend. Peace sign emoji.

Stormy: Love you chica. Have fun. Call me tomorrow to tell me all about it.

Skye: Same here. I know your roommate. She's AWESOME.

Skye: Love you.

Abi: :) Love you both.

The car slowed, and I looked up to see Jon turning onto an access road that looked like it hadn't been repaved in decades.

"What is this?" I asked.

"We're not there yet."

"Good."

"What happened to 'anywhere's good with me'?"

I laughed. "Did I say that?"

He rolled his eyes at me and kept driving. "That's what I thought."

When he turned again, we were on a dirt road,

dust billowing behind Jon's car. Rows and rows of crops passed outside my window. "We are officially in BFE. The middle of nowhere. The boonies. The—"

"I get it, I get it!" Jon laughed. "I heard the team does practices out here sometimes. Thought we could check it out."

A nervous flutter swept through my stomach at the mention of our new team, replacing my humor from earlier. We were collegiate athletes now. Wow. But you would think Upton would have better facilities. "We practice in a corn field?"

"I mean, I think we do our long runs along the road," Jon said. "It has lots of hills, and some big donor to the college owns this land."

There was a turnoff alongside the road that was too big to be a trail but too small to be a real parking lot. Slowly, he took his car off the gravel and onto the area carved into the field. He got out of the car and went to the trunk. I stood beside my door, taking it in. The midday sun beat down on us, every bit as hot as I'd expect it to be in August. Beads of sweat already formed on my skin, a bare echo of what would be there if our coaches had us run out here anytime soon.

Jon closed the trunk and walked my way, a bag

slung over his shoulder. When he reached me, he took my hand in his.

"You sure you don't mind sweaty hands?" I asked.

He lifted our interlaced fingers and kissed right below my knuckles. "Is that what I'm calling you now? Because if so, I love *Sweaty Hands*."

I giggled and shoved him away, but his hand stayed latched in mine.

"How do you know it's you sweating?" he asked.

"I just know."

He shook his head. "What do you think of Anika?"

"She seems nice." I shrugged. "I don't really know her yet. What about Kyle?"

"Seems cool," Jon said. "He's out for the football team."

"Ah."

"Weird that we got put together, huh?" he asked.

"The weirdest. Skye says she knows Anika."

"That's cool. You'll have to ask her for all of Anika's deep, dark secrets."

I winked at him. "One step ahead of you."

"You usually are. Thank God." He winked right back.

I laughed, even though he was ridiculous. And wrong.

He'd beaten me to a first real relationship. Had college figured out first. Healed from his trauma first. Knew his passion first. And with all of his comments about the *other* kind of passion, I couldn't help but be glad he hadn't lost his virginity yet. We had to be level on *some* playing field.

Jon just seemed so evolved. So comfortable in his own skin. Even though I knew I was still healing, I craved that kind of self-confidence, the kind that rarely cracked or faltered. Was desperate for it.

Almost as much as I was desperate for some shade and a massive glass of ice water.

I fanned my face with my free hand. "How far are we walking?"

The sound of vehicles from the nearby road had already faded, and we were now surrounded by sparse trees and a blanket of patchy grass growing in dapples of sunlight.

"I'm just looking for..." His eyes lit up. "There." He pointed at an area with no distinguishable features, as far as I could tell, and veered off the path.

"What?" I asked, nearly stumbling over a root.

"Two trees close enough together for this." He patted his duffle bag. "I brought a hammock."

My lips lifted into an easy smile. Jon, me, and a hammock? Talk about paradise.

Here in the shade, the temperature felt at least twenty degrees cooler, and a soft breeze had this little spot feeling almost comfortable.

I watched Jon as he put up the hammock, my eyes following his lean arms and shoulder muscles flexing through his thin T-shirt as he stretched and twisted. Sweat darkened his light brown hair and dripped down the curve of his chin. I wanted to kiss the drops, taste the saltiness, feel his skin under my lips.

He tested the straps, pushed the hammock back and forth, and then flopped into the fold, swinging rapidly and then slowing down.

I smiled at him, and he opened his arms wide, an invitation for me to claim my spot. He didn't need to ask twice. I fell into his arms, into his warmth, and snuggled in.

"This is perfect," I breathed, settling into the feeling of pure bliss.

His lips touched the top of my head, feather light, and he let out a contented breath.

We rocked back and forth for a little bit before Jon said, "I need to tell you something."

My heart froze at those words, and my entire body tensed. "What?"

Jon must have sensed my nerves because he kissed my head again, right where my hair met my forehead. Once, twice, three times. And then he said into my hair, "Remember where we were a year ago?"

I nodded cautiously. I'd been in my parents' house, living in the real-world version of hell, ruled by two demons who had devils of their own to answer for. Jon had been in Woodman, starting his senior year. A life with him—or someone like him—had been nowhere on my radar. It was a future as laughable as me walking on the moon.

He spoke softly into my hair. "I was just going through the motions... school, cross-country, home, sleep. And then you sat next to me on the bus." He kissed my temple, and my skin heated under his mouth. "You were so scared. I could see it in your eyes, even though you were trying to be strong, and I was...lost." He sighed. "I don't know how, but I knew I *needed* you. In a way I'd never needed anyone before, and it scared me."

He'd never told me that before. Confusion brought my eyebrows together, and I lifted up to look at him. "What are you trying to say?"

"I'm trying to say I'm sorry." With his eyes some-where in the past, he brushed a few loose strands of hair back behind my ears. "You know when you're on the verge of right where you're supposed to be, and you feel like you're not good enough?"

I recognized it as if I'd given birth to it. Every second, every moment of my life since moving to Woodman to live with Grandma, I felt that way. I lived with a woman who loved me, was in a relation-ship with *Jon Scoller*, had a track scholarship at a D1 college, good friends I group texted with. It was everything I'd dreamed of when I was locked in my room, burying my feelings in layers of comfort food, attempting to escape my parents.

Jon sighed. "The more I got to know you—fell in love with you—the more scared I became. I thought if I was the one to push you away, if I went another direction, dated another girl, I could end how I felt about you on my own terms, rather than watch it all blow up in my face. I almost lost everything. This."

I shook my head, remembering him going on morning runs with me behind Denise's back. My heart ached at his story. I wanted his words to be true. It would explain so much, take away so much pain from how we came together—and stayed apart.

"Abi..." He waited for me to look at him, and

when I did, he reached into his pocket and removed a thin golden ring set with blue stones.

I stared at him, open-mouthed.

"It's a promise ring," he said. "I'm sorry for how I acted when I was afraid. But I'm not afraid anymore, not of us. I want college to be a new start for us, and I want you to know, no matter what, I'm all in."

I slipped it on, and as I stared into the glittering stones, I couldn't help but see that I wore Jon's heart, right on my finger.

CHAPTER TWENTY

I'D CHANGED my outfit twice since waking up, and it was only eight in the morning. My hair was already frizzing, and I'd put more eyeliner on one eye than the other, making me look permanently winky no matter how much I tried to fix the situation.

Anika had left half an hour earlier, having an early class, and this room still wasn't big enough to hold all my angst.

Three knocks sounded on my door, and I checked to see who was on the other side.

Jon stood there, freshly showered, gorgeous, and as if he wasn't perfect enough, he was holding two cups of coffee.

I swung the door open to the welcome sight, giving him a frazzled grin.

"Thought you might need a little pick-me-up," he said.

I stood on my tiptoes and kissed his cheek. "Then what's the coffee for?"

He chuckled low and handed me a cup. "Cinnamon and honey, just like you like it."

I took it and stood back in front of the mirror, then eyed the shorts and T-shirt I had on my bed. Did jeans and a nice blouse on the first day of classes say I was trying too hard? Would I sweat too much on the walk?

Jon took my free hand and pulled me close. "Stop overthinking it." His lips found mine in a soft kiss. "You look amazing."

I tugged at my shirt. "Are you sure? I—"

"Abi." He ran his thumb over my bottom lip. "You're perfect."

I couldn't argue with that. More like I wouldn't argue when we could be kissing instead. So that's exactly what I did.

He groaned against my lips. "Abi, we have to go to class."

"Fine," I whined. I had to give myself some distance, so I grabbed my bag and keys and followed him into the hallway.

A few girls slipped by us, and I caught their eyes

following the lean lines of Jon's body. The hallway turned red, just for a moment. Until I could take a breath and remember he was my boyfriend. No one else's.

We walked together out of the building, holding hands until we had to go separate ways. Him to philosophy, me to an intro communications class. As our fingers slipped apart, he said, "I'll see you at practice tonight."

My lips twitched, despite the nerves brewing in my gut. "See you then."

The classroom building loomed before me, all brick and hard edges. I stared up at it, trying not to look as lost as I felt in front of all the other students passing by.

Next to me, I heard a couple of girls in running shorts and baggy sorority T-shirts laughing about how all the freshmen had dressed up. I tugged at my blouse, wishing I'd gone with the other outfit. But I couldn't change now.

I passed through the doors, hitching my thumbs through the straps of my backpack. The room numbers didn't make sense—237 was at one end of the hall and 239 at the complete opposite side. What "educated" person had designed this?

When I finally made it to the room, the professor

was already talking. She gave me a pointed look and handed me a syllabus.

"Now," she said, turning back to the class, "would be a great time to cover the section on punctuality."

If I could disappear into the ugly blue carpet, I would. Instead, I attempted to simultaneously find a seat and not make eye contact with anyone. The only open chairs were right up front. I slid into one and leaned over to get my notebook, letting my hair cover my face.

Great start, Abi.

But then someone else came into the classroom. I wasn't the only person who'd been a little lost.

I kept my eyes down as whoever it was took the open seat next to me.

"Hey," he whispered, even though we were right up front.

I peeked at him through my hair, seeing bright blue eyes and the same wavy brown hair from move-in day. I couldn't help the eye-roll that followed. Just my luck.

"What's your problem?" he asked, smirking.

I cleared my mind of his eyes and the way his lips turned up at the corners, leaving a dimple in his left cheek. "Yellow bug? Move-in day?"

He looked puzzled.

Was he playing dumb or actually stupid? "You cut me off in the drop-off line?"

"Technically, that was my cousin," he whispered. "I'm Eric."

The professor cleared her throat. "And now the syllabus section about disrupting class."

Eric's cheeks went red as he faced forward. I realized I should be doing the same.

A couple of minutes later, though, a slip of paper landed on my desk.

His phone number.

CHAPTER TWENTY-ONE

I DIDN'T KNOW WHY, but I kept the note. I slipped it in the front pocket of my backpack and carried it around with me all day, feeling guilty about doing so but excited to have it.

What was wrong with me?

Maybe it was because he'd actually seen me when this campus seemed designed to promote anonymity. Classrooms with hundreds of students, sidewalks separated with "lanes," people constantly walking with their headphones in and heads down.

In high school, I'd always felt like there was a giant, flashing bully-me arrow pointing straight at my head, and I had to *work* to be invisible. Here, I blended into the sea of girls in their too-short shorts and guys who made speed walking to classes a sport.

Aside from Eric and the professor's pointed comments, no one seemed to notice me the entire day. When I finally set my backpack down in my dorm to change into clothes for practice, the number had me wound so tightly, I wished he had never given it to me. Almost.

I used the walk to the training center to try and clear my mind. Music by Dorian Gray filled my earbuds, soft chords filling my mind. My thoughts turned to track and everything I could accomplish, doing it with Jon at my side just like I'd dreamed. Jon always made a good distraction—the perfect obsession.

As I approached the indoor track, getting in the zone became easier. I'd been practicing, training, for a year now. I loved the way running and eating a healthier diet had transformed my body into some-thing strong and capable. When Jon wasn't available, when he was with Denise, running was always there. My diet and new healthy lifestyle were there. Even if Jon realized he could do better, I would have this. This center, the facility, the team, was the piece of home I was most excited to bring with me.

"Abi!" Jon yelled. "Abi!" From the tone of his voice, I could tell he'd been trying to get my attention for a little while.

I pulled out an earbud and turned to see him jogging toward me. I smiled at him as he crossed the last several feet and took me in his arms, squeezing me. "It's weird not having any classes with you," he said.

I smiled up at him. "How was your day?"

He let go of me and shrugged. "I'll let you know after practice."

Nerves bubbled inside me as I wrapped up my earbuds and put my phone in my pocket. I had no idea what to expect from the first track practice—or any practice for that matter. If the workouts from the summer were any indication, they'd be grueling and on the verge of torturous.

"Want to get supper afterwards?" he asked. "Lick our wounds?"

I nodded. "One wound-licking date, coming up."

We quieted at the door as we joined the group of athletes. Our coaches began the practice by separating the girls' and boys' teams and going over rules for the season. We had to sign a code of conduct agreement.

Coach Cadence laid out how the rest of the week would go, with weight training every other day at the crack of dawn and long runs for the distance runners in the evenings. Then she told us we had to make an appointment with the athletic nutritionist.

My eyes lit up. I'd been going off of tips learned online and in Grandma's magazines for the last year. I couldn't wait to get actual personalized advice.

And then they gave us more gear than I knew what to do with. Collegiate branded shorts, T-shirts, tennis shoes, jackets, heavy winter coats, water bottles, even headbands.

My eyes widened at the spread. I'd never owned so much name-brand clothing. I couldn't wait to feel the way the fabric would ripple over my skin, feather soft.

All that excitement left when Coach Cadence told us to get on the line of the big indoor football field and start running. She worked us, running line after line, until my legs could hardly carry me anymore. The other girls there were athletic, more so than me, and even they looked about ready to fall over.

When Coach finally told us we could go home, I was worried I wouldn't make it the entire way. I picked up my bag and started walking toward the door on shaking legs.

"Abi," she called in her heavy Ethiopian accent.

I waited for her to walk to me, because there was no way I'd log extra steps, not right now.

She gave me an approving nod. "Good work today. I see what Coach Rodham saw in you at that meet."

My heart lifted at her affirmation. "Really?"

She smiled, white teeth shining against her beautiful dark skin. "We have a lot of work to do, but we'll get you there. Make sure to eat a good meal and ice up. Okay?"

"I will," I said.

Her words gave me a strange blend of buoyancy and pressure. What did she mean that we had a lot of work to do? Would I be dragging the team down? Was that just a nice way of telling me not to get my hopes up?

I wished something else could distract me. That was, until I saw a letter on my desk next to a sticky note from Anika that said she had picked up our mail.

This letter wasn't forwarded, but addressed to me, at my new address. No return label. This one was stamped from Austin.

With shaking hands, I opened it and looked at the now-familiar block lettering.

You can't outrun everything.

My heart sped, along with my breathing. Thank God Anika wasn't here to see me fall apart as I ran to the door and made sure it was locked, panic making every part of me shake. What was going on? Who was this and how had they gotten my new address?

I fell into my desk chair, no longer able to stand on trembling ankles. The only people I'd sent my address to were Grandma and my friends in the group text.

I grasped at my straw of hope that this was just an ongoing prank. And not a very funny one.

My fingers rattled against my phone screen as I thumbed out a text to the friend group.

Abi: I'm bored. Anyone been up to any pranks lately?

It was meant to sound like a joking conversation starter. I didn't want Jon to know or ask what had me riled up. After tonight's practice, I honestly didn't have the energy for long, drawn-out conversations or speculations that got us nowhere and left me even more terrified.

A few bubbles popped up on the screen.

Michele: Nope.

Evan: What's a prank?

Andrew: None that you'd want to know about. ;)
Definitely none in the community shower.

Skye: Shut up Andrew!

Frank: You go man!

Macy: Can we start a girls-only chat?

Frank: Can I watch?

Leanne: Grow up.

Stormy: What she said.

Andrew: Can we revisit Frank's text?

I sighed and sent Stormy a text in our own chat.

Abi: Hey, I know we were going to talk tonight, but I'm not feeling up to it. Rough practice. Talk to you tomorrow?

I didn't wait for her answer before turning off my phone and putting it in my desk drawer, along with the letter. Coach Cadence had said to eat well tonight, but I couldn't imagine adding anything to the acid brewing in my stomach. Instead, I killed the lights, crawled up to my bunk with weak limbs, and curled under my covers until darkness shut out every thought and fear and ache I had.

CHAPTER TWENTY-TWO

ANIKA'S ALARM clock woke me the next morning, and thank God it had because I had fifteen minutes to get across campus to the training center for a weightlifting session. Coach had gone over what would happen if we were late, and it was exponentially more unpleasant than practice the night before.

I opened the door to find Jon racing down the hallway.

"What are you doing?" I asked.

He gasped out a breath. "You're going to be late. I was worried you'd slept in."

"No, I didn—" Then it hit me. Jon and I were supposed to eat supper together last night in the dining hall to talk about practice. I'd totally blown him off. "Jon, I'm so sorry about last night."

He batted away my comment, then grabbed my hand and started down the hallway. "Let's go. We're going to be late."

"Really," I said, not ready to let it drop. My legs protested right along with me—for different reasons —but soon my muscles loosened up.

He chuckled, his arms working at his sides. "I came by and Anika let me in. You were *out*." He laughed again. "You're a loud snorer, by the way."

My cheeks warmed, even though I had more to be embarrassed about than Jon hearing me snoring. But still. "I'll make it up to you tonight."

He turned his head toward me, waggling his eyebrows. "In the community showers?"

Even running, I managed to hit his arm, to which he laughed.

"You're just as bad as they are," I accused.

"I never said I wasn't."

We jogged into the weight room, then headed to different ends of the rows and rows of equipment with our teams. I'd never seen so many weight plates, benches, or squat racks before in my life. To be fair, my extent of exercise was pretty limited to body-weight movements.

Coach Cadence had the distance runners move through a series of lifts she said would keep our muscles toned and give us what we needed to be strong in the final stretches of races. That translated to a series of lifts that made it impossible to put my arms over my head or stand without staggering to my feet.

"Holy shit," the girl next to me muttered, hanging her head over her knees and then sitting on a weight bench.

"Right?" I considered sitting next to her but thought better of it. If I sat down, I wouldn't be able to stand up again.

She turned her head back and up to face me, revealing her bright red skin and shining nose ring. "You're Abi, right?"

"Yeah," I replied, feeling guilty I didn't know her name yet.

"Nikki," she offered.

I smiled. Or did something in the family. How had lifting made my face tired too?

This was the part of meeting people that always felt the most awkward. Most people started with boring things—hometown, major, "fun" fact. And of course everyone immediately forgot that meaningless information anyway. I wanted to know something real about Nikki, but I didn't know how to ask.

"You up for an ice bath?" she asked.

I thought of Jon telling me about it over the summer. It didn't sound any more appealing now than it had then. But I'd do anything to make this ache go away. "Will it make me feel better?"

She snorted, making her nose ring wiggle. "Hell yeah."

"Sign me up."

She told me to meet her at the entrance to my residence hall after supper that evening, to which I happily agreed.

Jon found me on the way out, and we started walking—slowly—to our dorm rooms together.

"We good for supper tonight? Or are you having a big bowl of snore soup again?" he teased.

I gave him a weak shove.

"And for dessert, maybe some s'nores?"

I rolled my eyes. "You're harshing my mallow."

He buried his face in my shoulder and wiggled his nose side to side, right against the ticklish spot on my collarbone.

"Stop," I cried. "Laughing hurts my abs."

To which he laughed.

And I laughed more. Until it hurt even more.

When the giggles subsided, I said, "Yes, I'm good for supper."

"So." Jon rubbed his neck. That was his tell

when he was nervous about something. It set me on edge.

"Yeah?"

"Well, one of the guys on the team invited everyone out tonight. Team bonding."

I raised an eyebrow. "Are you asking me permission?"

"What?" He shook his head. "No, I mean, maybe? Is it okay? I told them I would see what you were doing first."

My stomach sank while my heart lifted. Why did I feel both pleased and rejected at the same time? Maybe because I could tell how much he wanted to go.

I had plans too, I reminded myself. "That's fine. I'm actually hanging out with one of the girls from the team."

Jon's lips spread in a grin. "Really?"

"Are you really that surprised someone would want to hang out with me?" I was only partly joking.

"No, I mean, of course not. I just knew you were worried about making friends."

I was such a jerk. "I'm sorry. I'm just...tired." And stressed. And scared. I glanced over my shoulder, just to make sure no one was following us. Or had overheard my plans for later.

His brows furrowed. "Is everything okay?"

Forcing a smile, I nodded.

We were getting close to the dorms anyway.

"I'll see you later," I said and kissed his cheek.

Anything that was going on with me could wait. It wasn't worth ruining that perfect smile and making that troubled look cross his eyes.

CHAPTER TWENTY-THREE

JUST LIKE PROMISED, I waited for Nikki at the entrance to my dorms. I wasn't sure what one wore for an ice bath, but I'd dressed in my one-piece swimsuit under shorts and a T-shirt. I definitely wasn't skinny-dipping. Or ice cubing. Whatever the hell you called it.

She pulled up in a beat-up pickup. One girl rode in the passenger seat, and one sat on a wheel well in the bed.

"Hop in the back!" Nikki called.

Too tired to worry about riding without seatbelts or where we were going, I threw my bag in and climbed over the tailgate. At least a plastic mat covered the floor and it was relatively clean.

As Nikki pulled away, the girl in the back

grinned at me, showing off pink braces. I thought I recognized her as one of the sprinters. "Hey, I'm Jayne," she said.

"Abi." I smiled back, but it probably looked more like a grimace. "Do you know where we're going?"

"Yeah." She grinned. "Nikki's dad set up a stock tank with ice water for us. It's about thirty minutes from here."

"Like, a tank, for cattle?"

She laughed. I was beginning to wonder if all she did was laugh and smile. "Yeah," she said. "It's clean, though. They just have it in their backyard. And her mom usually brings us these bomb recovery shakes. You'll love her."

I forgave her for using the word "bomb." Probably because her smile was so contagious I already felt my mood lifting and my nerves easing.

"That's awesome," I said.

"What classes are you in?" she asked.

Over the next half hour, I found out Jayne was a nursing major, a sophomore, from North Carolina, and that she wanted to work in a children's oncology unit someday. That she had a little cousin who died from osteosarcoma—a bone cancer—and that she broke up with her boyfriend to come here on scholarship. The real stuff.

It made me wonder what her smile was hiding or if she was actually that happy. That dedicated to living life to its fullest.

Nikki parked the truck next to an old farmhouse lined with blooming flower beds and vines climbing white lattices. A black and white dog came running up to the pickup and jumped on Nikki the second she got out.

After giving it a scratch and pretending to be annoyed that it slobbered all over her face, she started toward the house. I followed her and the other girls to the back porch, where a silver tank waited, brimming with ice.

I came to a stop beside Nikki, staring at it.

"Welcome to paradise," she said.

The other girls walked to a bench on the porch, pulling off their shirts and shorts to reveal sports bras and spandex. I felt a little over (under?) dressed in my swimsuit, but I went with it, too tired to be self-conscious. No one commented on my attire anyway. They were already slipping into the ice, shouting expletives as they sank lower into the freezing cold water.

I followed suit, trying to resist the urge to jump out and have them committed. The liquid felt like a million needles poking into my skin. This was torture on par with line sprints and pop quizzes.

"You ladies watch your mouths!" a southern voice called from the porch, but there was humor in her voice.

A woman who looked almost exactly like Nikki, but only slightly older, came out carrying a tray with four cocktail glasses that had umbrellas sticking out and fresh pineapple slices wedged over the edges.

She smiled at me—with her eyes and her mouth —and said, "Now I recognize Jayne and Mollie, but I haven't met you yet."

"Abi," I said over chattering teeth and took a glass from her. "Thanks."

"Cheers, darlin'."

I lifted the cup and then cautiously took a sip. Jayne hadn't mentioned alcohol when she told me about the "recovery" shakes, but I couldn't be too certain.

All I could taste, though, was a blend of fruit and what I guessed was protein powder.

Nikki groaned and sank down to her chin with her eyes closed. "God, getting started again is such a bitch."

The other girls mumbled their agreement.

"Tell me it gets better," I begged.

"Oh yeah," Mollie said. "Like a million times better. Especially when meets start."

A relieved sigh escaped my lips, making steam pour over the uneven surface.

"I saw that." Nikki laughed. "Coach Cadence is rough, but she'll make you the best you can be."

"Yeah?" I asked.

"This will be my third year on the team, and she got me to place at nationals last year," Nikki said. "I was nowhere near that level when I started."

Mollie nodded. "I kind of wish I had her for a coach."

"Coach Mel isn't bad," Jayne offered.

"Yeah, but not great like Cadence," Mollie retorted.

Nikki's mouth twisted to the side. "If she recruited you for the team, Abi, it means something."

I ran my shivering hand over the bumpy surface of the water, making ice cubes rattle against each other. "Actually, the boys' coach recruited me."

"Huh?" Mollie asked.

"It's kind of a long story."

"Spill," Nikki said.

So I told them about Jon and how he'd gotten his coach to come to our meet and how it had gone from there. How he'd worked a deal for us both to go to

Upton because Jon refused to run there if I didn't get admitted. We were a package deal.

My smile was bittersweet. "He said he'd run at a community college if that's what it took for us to be together." I had felt guilty he was sacrificing for me, but now I had the double consequence of feeling like I didn't belong amongst the other runners. Like I hadn't earned it. They were all so talented.

The girls gushed, though.

"That is so sweet," Jayne said.

Mollie nodded. "I'd kill for my boyfriend to care that much."

Nikki whistled. "Boy must be crazy about you."

I decided to voice my fear, even if I couldn't meet their eyes. "I can't help feeling like I don't belong here, though."

"No," Nikki countered, her voice firm. "You wouldn't be here if Cadence wasn't okay with it. And I saw you in practice. You have some real potential. You've just got to get your form down and your diet on point."

I wanted so badly for her words to be true. If that was what it took—hard work and good nutrition, I could do it. I promised myself I would, for the team, for Jon, for me.

After half an hour in the ice bath, we got out and

dried off. Back in high school, I might have wanted to make a night of it, but now I was spent. My body thoroughly used and ready for a break.

Judging by the way the other girls moved slowly, stiffly, they felt the same way. Nikki dropped us back at the dorms around midnight. Anika was already asleep, so I took my things to the community bathroom to change and get ready for bed.

As I took in my reflection, I couldn't believe how much I'd changed in the last year. I still remembered looking in the mirror at Grandma's and hating everything I saw. My face wasn't round now. It had lines and contours. My collarbones actually showed on my shoulders. My stomach wasn't flat, but it was strong. I still had the same dishwater blue eyes though, the same mousy blond hair. I considered getting highlights, but I didn't have that kind of money, and I couldn't imagine asking Grandma for more than she'd already given me.

With a sigh, I stepped into a stall and changed into pajama shorts and a tank top. Somehow, I managed to do all of that without dropping anything in the toilet—impressive considering how completely exhausted I was. Thankfully, I didn't have class the next morning. Just my appointment with the nutritionist.

When I got into the room, sending a sliver of light over Anika's bed, she rolled over. I hurriedly shut the door as silently as I could, hoping I wouldn't wake her. After a few moments, her breathing turned heavy again, and I continued to my bed, bringing my phone with me.

Curled into my pillows and comforter, I checked my messages for a goodnight text from Jon, but instead saw nothing. My fingers itched to text him, but I needed to prove to myself, to him, that I wasn't as desperate as I felt. I fell asleep aching for him, but knowing I couldn't do anything about it. Not right now.

CHAPTER TWENTY-FOUR

THE NUTRITIONIST HELD the door open, her sleeveless blouse showing off toned arms. "Come in, Abi."

I walked into the small office, papered entirely with photos of her, a handsome guy, and two small children, along with Upton gear.

"I'm Deborah," she said.

I nodded. What else was there to say to that?

"I have some ideas for us, but I wanted to hear from you first. What are your goals for the season?"

"To deserve my spot here," I said. "I want to be the best I can be. I worked hard in high school, but I know I have a lot to learn."

"And I'm here to help you do that. What you did

in high school may have gotten you here, but it isn't going to take you to the next level."

I nodded eagerly. "I'm ready." I couldn't wait to get her take on this. To do what I'd promised myself I would the night before.

"Let's start with your existing diet." She handed me a few slips of paper with slots for every meal. "Go ahead and fill out everything you've eaten for the last few days. Every cookie, every snack, every mustard packet, I want to know about it."

The thought of putting my flaws on display for her made my stomach turn, but I needed this to get better.

I began writing my breakfasts—usually grape-fruit or eggs and skim milk. My lunches—some salad with protein, no dressing. And supper...my pen hovered over the page. I hadn't even eaten supper the last two days, being so preoccupied with the letters and Jon and practice. I could have put my "typical" meal, but I decided to be honest and left them blank.

I handed the pages back to her and sat on the edge of my chair as I waited for her to read them over. I didn't know what I'd expected, but it wasn't the furrow that crossed her brow.

"Are you sure you're not forgetting something?" she asked.

I shook my head. "No, the first day I gave you is what I usually do. I've had a rough couple of days, so that's why I missed dinner."

She set the pages down and got out a laminated sheet and calculator. The keys crackled as she began a calculation. "Even with supper..." Her frown deepened. "You're getting *maybe* a thousand calories in a day. Maybe."

Suddenly, I felt two hundred pounds again with the scale staring back at me, reminding me of my shortcomings. "I'm not starving myself or anything."

Her lips settled into a frown, and she pushed her glasses into her hair. "Abi..." She gave me an even look. "Have you ever struggled with anorexia?"

I couldn't help it. I laughed. "Me?" That was the most ridiculous thing I'd heard all day. "I'm the last person you should be asking that. I weigh a hundred and forty pounds. I'm not a stick by any means."

"You know, you don't have to be emaciated to have an eating disorder." Without so much as a smile, she asked, "Have you always weighed that much?"

The seat suddenly felt uncomfortable, and I shifted. "No. I used to weigh more."

"What did you weigh?"

I bit the inside of my cheek. "A little over two hundred pounds."

Her eyebrows lifted, but she quickly lowered them. "You have worked hard to be here, haven't you?"

"You have no idea." It was the truth. I'd been going on early morning runs, doing the track workouts Coach sent home, every single day.

"Do you ever do extra workouts on top of practices?"

"I mean, yeah? Sometimes." What kind of question was that? I assumed everyone else playing sports at the college level had done the same.

"Abi, can I level with you?"

Feeling exposed, I folded my arms over my chest. "Sure?"

"With how much you eat and exercise, you are on the borderline for having an eating disorder."

The words sent a shock through my system. How had I gone from multiple desserts a day to having an eating disorder? And even worse, it minimized all the work I'd put in to get myself here. "So just because I've worked hard to lose weight, I'm anorexic?"

"No. Because you eat little compared to how hard you're working, you're on the borderline. You can't do that as a college athlete," she said. "Your coaches' practices are more than enough to get you in top physical shape, but only if you have the energy your body needs to build muscle and recover. No more skipping meals. No extra workouts, unless your coach gives them to you. And for the love of God, use some salad dressing. Vinaigrette at least."

But I hardly heard her words. My mind was still stuck on the words "eating disorder." Did she have any idea how hard it was to choose salad when everyone else was eating pizza? How hard I'd worked to keep my sugar intake low, even switching fruits for those lower in carbohydrates?

Did she know she was just echoing everything my mom told me before she spat at me and maimed my face?

I stood up and put my backpack over my shoulder, livid. "I do not have an eating disorder," I fumed, voice shaking from anger. Now I didn't even see her. I saw my mom and her sunken eyes, her lips curled back with distain. "I have been dedicated to being the best I can be, and for you to even insinuate..." I couldn't finish the sentence.

Her eyes widened. "Abi, I said borderline." She stood up too, holding out a packet of papers. "Look, I know being a college student is a big change, especially when you're in a sport as demanding as distance running. Why don't you try this meal plan I put together for you this week. If it doesn't work, come see me again."

I turned my head away from her, not able to look at her without wanting to scream. No matter how far away I got from my mother, her words chased me everywhere I went. I bit down on my cheek, chewing hard just to keep my mouth shut.

"Okay?" she asked.

I released the inside of my cheek, tasting blood. "Do I have a choice?"

"No."

"Then, I'll be seeing you again," I said and got out of there as fast as I could.

CHAPTER TWENTY-FIVE

THE MEETING with the team nutritionist followed my every thought for the next two days. I should have been enjoying my first week of college, making new friends in class, struggling through track practice just like everyone else, and here I was, sitting across from my perfect boyfriend in the dining hall, staring down at one of *Deborah's* suggested meals.

All of the research I'd done showed to cut fat and simple carbs in lieu of lean protein and complex carbohydrates. I had a salad, ranch dressing, a grilled chicken thigh with juice dripping from it, green beans with bacon, and a hefty hunk watermelon, which was one of the fruits with the most sugars.

"What's going on?" Jon asked. "You've been off."

I twirled my fork around one of the fatty strings of bacon. "Just tired, I guess."

His hand covered mine over the fork. "Not just now. You've been different for a while now. Since graduation."

My eyebrows furrowed. "What do you mean?"

He lifted his hands with his shrug. "I don't know. You just seem more...closed off. Like there's something you're not telling me. You put that wall back up."

I chewed at my straw, trying not to fall apart. If only he knew all the messiness, the brokenness I was holding back. He deserved so much better that all of that, with his perfect life back home. Before he knew me, he had the life. Perfect, loving parents. Amazing talent at a sport that left him with plenty of options for friends and girlfriends. But then I came in with my past and vomited it all over his easy life.

"I'm just me," I said instead.

"But what about us?" he asked.

"Us is...everything to me."

"Is it?" he asked, like he wasn't sure.

How could he not be sure?

"It is," I promised.

"But every time I even mention being intimate, you freeze." For a second, I saw his real feelings, the hurt and rejection lying underneath his easygoing surface.

"Is that what you want?" I asked. "To have…" I couldn't even say the word sex out loud in the dining hall with people going about their perfectly average lives all around us. Which was probably a sure sign I wasn't even close to ready.

No one had ever been interested in me enough for me to really think about it. To get close.

And the thought—the possibility—of becoming a parent? How would I even know how to do that? It wasn't like I had shining examples to go off of.

Jon rubbed his arm, looking at me under his lashes. "I want you. In the morning when your breath smells like an old gym bag. When you have sweat dripping down your neck in track practice and your face is all red."

My cheeks were red now, alright. I barely stifled the urge to cup my hand over my mouth and check my breath.

He reached out and rubbed his thumb over my cheek. "When you're self-conscious because I just brought up morning breath and track practice."

I managed a smile, but it didn't stay long. "It's not an easy decision for me," I admitted. "It means a lot. I need to be sure."

But that was the wrong thing to say, because his entire face fell. "You're not sure about us."

He didn't say it like a question. It was a statement in his eyes. An indisputable fact.

"That's not what I said."

"How would I know, though?" he asked. "This is the first real conversation we've had about it. And I know that's not all that's been bothering you lately."

I couldn't keep his gaze, shifting my eyes to the table.

"That's what I thought," he said, standing up.

Doing the same, I asked, "Where are you going?"

"I'm meeting with some people from class to work on homework." A frown marred his features. "I'm not going to make you talk to me about anything." He gestured between the two of us. "But that's what a relationship is, Abi. We talk. We figure things out. I thought that's what you wanted with me."

The broken pieces of me spread apart, dangerously close to breaking. "What do you mean? Of course it's what I want."

I went to stand too. I needed to go to him and hold him and kiss away any part of him that thought I didn't want to be with him in every sense of the word.

But he held his hand out, stopping me. "Finish your food," he said. "You barely touched it."

"I'm not hungry now," I countered. "I want to talk about it."

"I don't." He sighed. "Not now. I'll see you later."

As he walked away, I scrabbled at the thrown-together pieces of my heart, trying to keep from falling apart all over again. Feeling lost, I sat back down. My gaze focused in and out on the plate in front of me as panic rose in my chest.

I put my head in my hands. I was an idiot. I should have told Jon about my meeting with the nutritionist, about the letters, but I'd been too scared of what those things said about me. Honestly, I still was. Would he want to be with someone who was so much drama?

"Abi?" someone said.

I lifted my gaze into bright blue eyes lined with thick, dark lashes. My mind went to the slip of paper still in my backpack, the neat writing marking his phone number. "Eric. What are you doing here?"

He held up his tray. "Oh, you know, catching beautiful girls by surprise with my wit and boyishly good looks."

Despite the anxiety rolling in my chest, I smiled.

"See?" he said. "It's working."

I rolled my eyes. "Is it?"

"I don't know. Are you going to let me sit down?"

I chewed on my lip. For whatever reason, I nodded. Maybe I just needed a distraction. Someone who I wasn't failing.

He slid into the seat across from me and immediately dug into his cheeseburger. Eric wasn't ripped or toned or even lean, but he was strong. It made me wonder, did he used to play sports? Did he grow up on a farm? Did he go to the rec center and play pickup ball games for fun?

"You think too much," he said, using a wad of napkins to wipe a glob of ketchup off his chin.

The ridiculousness of it all was exactly the distraction I needed. "You're a mess."

"Yeah, but you can't spell mess without..." His eyes turned toward the ceiling. "Yeah, I don't know where I was going with that."

My laugh came even easier this time.

"So what's your story?" he asked.

"What's yours?"

A shadow crossed his eyes but quickly passed. "We don't need to talk about it." He nodded toward my chest. At the Upton Track graphic on my shirt. "You're on the track team?"

I nodded. And for a second, I let myself pretend that's all there was to my story. That I had a normal family. A normal high school experience with a few dances, a few heartbreaks, and a few really good friends. Then I shrugged and let the dream live on a little longer. "That's about all there is."

His blue eyes narrowed, somewhere between fun and teasing. There was something else there I couldn't quite place. "You're being modest."

"Oh really?"

"Yeah," he said. "I bet you were...what, homecoming queen? Star of the track team? Made it to state but didn't medal? Broke some poor sap's heart when you came to college because you wanted to leave yourself open for..." He plucked at his shirt, winked a big blue eye at me. "New opportunities."

"You are full of yourself." I giggled.

"Maybe," he said. "But why aren't you?"

CHAPTER TWENTY-SIX

INSTEAD OF GOING BACK to my room, I called Stormy and took to one of the winding sidewalks around campus. It was getting colder outside, but I needed the space away from the four walls of my shared room.

She picked up within a few rings and gave me her regular greeting. "Hey, *chica.*"

"Hey." My voice came out shakier than I meant it to, and suddenly, everything about me, my life, felt shaky.

Jon and I never fought, not since we'd been together. And he never looked at me with disappointment in his eyes. I never had easy, flirting conversations with other guys. It shattered me.

"What's wrong?" Stormy asked, concern apparent in her tone.

I dropped my face in my hands and rubbed. "What isn't wrong?"

She let out a sympathetic laugh. "Why don't you start at the beginning, babe?"

So I did. And even though I'd only been in college a week, it took nearly an hour to tell her everything that had been going on. How Jon felt more distant than ever and that the nutritionist was off her rocker. But I made sure to tell Stormy the good things too, including my new almost-friends and the nice thing Coach Cadence said about me. I hesitated, considering if I should tell her about the notes.

"Wow, you've had a big week." She let out a small laugh. "All I've done since Monday is wait tables and binge watch *Riverdale* on Netflix."

The hurt in her voice was obvious. Stormy had problems of her own. She didn't need me to call and complain about what, on paper, looked like an amazing opportunity.

"Are you okay?" I asked.

"I don't know—I just...I..." She sighed.

"Are you sad you stayed in Woodman?"

"What do you think, Abi?" Frustration edged its

way into her tone. "I'm living with my mom and stepdad, waiting tables, trying to save enough money to get a place of my own. And then what? I get married, have kids, and never do anything for myself my entire life?"

My heart ached for her. "It doesn't have to be that way. You are one of the smartest people I know."

"Look, Abi," she said, a wall around her feelings again. "You got your fairy tale. Things worked out for you. They don't happen like that for everyone."

CHAPTER TWENTY-SEVEN

THE LINE WENT SILENT, and I slouched down on the bench, letting my head drop back over the backrest. There I went, blowing everything that mattered to me, yet again. I should have asked her about her life instead of going on about mine for an entire hour.

Mom's words echoed in my brain, crashing against my skull until all I could hear was her telling me I didn't deserve friends. That no matter what I did, I would be worthless.

I was having a hard time not believing her.

Still, I wasn't giving up. I hadn't lost sixty pounds, trained for hours a day, put myself out there and risked the ultimate heartbreak for nothing. I sent Jon a text and started back to my dorm.

Abi: I'm ready to talk when you are. I mean it.

After putting my phone in my pocket, I started back toward the tall dorm building, framed against the darkening sky. When I arrived, Anika was already in her bed, leaning against the wall with her legs dangling over the edge.

At the sound of the door opening, she closed the textbook in her lap and smiled at me. "How's it going?"

I blew a stray hair out of my face. "I've had better days. You?"

She shook her head. "I'm reading my textbook on my first Friday night of college. The outlook isn't great."

"What's Kyle doing?"

"Some team bonding thing." She shrugged.

I dropped my bag on the desk and fell into my chair. "Girl. We've got to do something about this."

"You sure?" Her eyes lit up. "What did you have in mind?"

Her reaction made me wonder if she felt as nervous and out of place as I did. Unfortunately, I was as clueless as she was about how to navigate college life.

"Um. I have no idea. Do you know of any parties going on?" Even as I said it, I cringed. Binge drinking at some random house didn't sound like a great time.

Her face mirrored mine. "Maybe a movie?"

Another bad idea. She knew it, and I did too. We could have done that back home.

"Do you know anyone older who goes here?" I asked.

Her expression turned stormy for a fraction of a second before she shook her head. "You? Maybe someone on the track team?"

"Yeah, but..." I kicked myself, realizing I hadn't even asked Nikki or the other girls for their numbers. I was so far out of the game, I wasn't even in the ticket line. How I managed to have a solid friend group at home, I didn't know. I shook my head.

"Anyone from class?" she asked.

My mind went to the slip of paper in my back-pack and the confident, funny guy it belonged to. "Kind of?"

She lifted her eyebrows.

"I mean, he gave me his number in class." Guilt wracked my stomach. "I haven't called him or anything."

Her eyes narrowed in a way that told me she knew there was more to the story, but she wasn't going to ask. Instead, she said, "Having guy friends isn't a crime, Abi."

I nodded toward her mirror and the cute guy in most of her pictures. "Like him?"

She smiled at his image. "That's Bran. The jerk went to community college and left me here." Her lips fell into a frown. "And Kyle's already so tied up in football."

"I hear that." We were only a week in, and it seemed like Jon and I would have to fight more than ever to make our relationship work. But after today, I didn't know if he was up for the challenge.

"What's Jon doing?" she asked.

"Working on homework with some friends." I tried to make it seem normal, like this wasn't the first Friday night in months we hadn't spent together.

"So you're calling that guy?" she asked.

Chewing on my lip, I nodded and reached into my backpack. My fingertips brushed the crisp fold of the notebook paper.

A gnawing feeling hit my stomach, like I shouldn't be doing this. But then I went to my message I sent Jon. He had seen it, and he'd chosen not to reply.

I typed in the new numbers, testing them, and held the phone to my ear.

"Hello?" he answered.

I closed my eyes. "Hey." But then I stalled. What could I say next to show that I wanted friendship, maybe some guidance, and nothing more?

"Abi?"

"How many girls did you give your number to the first week?"

"Let's say I had about a one in a hundred chance of getting it right."

I rolled my eyes. "Uh huh."

"What's up?"

I glanced at Anika, who was sitting on the edge of the bed now. "My friend and I are bored. Wondering if you had any ideas?"

"Is your friend hot?"

I rolled my eyes again. "You're lucky I'm not within arm's length."

"Uh huh." Even through the phone, his grin was apparent. "Do I have any ideas." He scoffed. "Meet me outside the dining hall in ten. Oh, and wear sneakers."

CHAPTER TWENTY-EIGHT

ERIC WAITED for us by the dining hall entrance. It was dark outside, but a nearby light pole cast a glow over his face, enhancing the planes and edges there. I still didn't know what he had in mind, but he wasn't dressed for a night on the town. No, it looked like he'd just gotten done working out at the rec. Minus the sweat.

He looked at Anika. "Is this the friend? She is hot."

If I thought I blushed badly, Anika was worse. By a hundred. She giggled awkwardly and shook her head. "I'm taken."

He made an exaggerated frown and shrugged. "I'll be patient."

She laughed—a real one this time—and said, almost to herself, "You remind me of my friend."

Since Anika seemed lost in memories, I asked, "So what's this mysterious plan?"

Instead of replying, Eric lifted an arm and pointed at the campus's bell tower. It rose from the library, looming even taller than the dorms.

My eyebrows came together. "What..."

I looked down at my shoes, then at Anika, who appeared to be just as panicked as I was.

"No," I said. "No. I could get kicked off the track team."

"Relax," Eric said, holding up a key. "I work for facilities. I'm *allowed*."

My shoulders relaxed, even if I only partly believed him. It was hard to tell when he was joking with that ornery look constantly gleaming in his eyes.

"I'm game," Anika said, surprising me. "What?" she questioned with a shrug. "It's not any worse than a grain elevator."

The cement silos on the outskirts of town came to mind. "You've climbed those?"

With a sheepish smile, she nodded.

"Come on." Eric started walking. "We're burning daylight."

"It's nighttime," I pointed out.

"And?"

I rolled my eyes at Anika and followed.

As we walked to the library, he pointed out the things no one told you on your campus tour. Like the fountain where if you got in, you'd be a virgin for life. Or the dorm window that looked different from all the others because some guy threw a microwave out of it last year. I found myself seeing the college in an entirely new light. It didn't seem so intimidating and pristine when he said things like that.

Eventually, we got to a solid metal door at the back of the library. There was a big padlock on it, even though the library was still open through the main entrance. Eric selected a key from what seemed like a hundred on his keyring, like he'd done this a million times before. The lock unlatched with a heaving clicking sound, and Eric led us into a shabby hallway that looked nothing like the rest of the campus. Already nerves lit my veins, the feeling of forbidden-ness setting me ablaze with adrenaline.

"Where are we?" Anika asked, her voice echoing off the cinderblock walls.

Eric started down the hallway. "This is the service entrance."

Following him, I scanned the walls and the signs by each door. They indicated books in storage, the boiler room, a bathroom. And that no one was allowed back here.

He stopped at an elevator and pushed the grubby up button. A grin shined on his face as he looked at us. "Ready to get high?"

I cringed. "That's a terrible pun." Still, I laughed.

Anika's laughter joined mine. "Seriously."

The door chimed open, and he stepped onto worn brown carpet. We followed him in, and the elevator suddenly felt much smaller than it actually was. I could smell Eric from here. *Feel* his presence. The cologne that was so different from Jon's. His body that was so broad, the opposite of Jon's lean frame. It just made me miss Jon that much more.

My heart hurt thinking of my phone, which still hadn't chimed. Jon should have been here with us. Exploring, going on adventures, seeing the campus like never before.

After ten floors, the elevator opened to a metal door that Eric had to unlock with one of his many keys.

When it slid open, we got the full view of the bell tower—the tarnished brass, brick walls and cement floors, and then all of campus and Austin spread before us.

"Wow," Anika breathed.

Wow was right. I stepped farther out onto the cement floor, eyes wide. We couldn't see the stars here, but the glittering lights of the city shined just as brightly. In contrast, the campus was a dark blanket cutting into the city with only a few lamps illuminating the sidewalk.

I rested my arms on the wall, wanting to take it all in for as long as I could.

Eric placed his folded arms just near enough to mine for them to touch, and the breeze lifted his hair as he looked at me. "What do you think?"

"Everything seems so small from here," I said.

His lips quirked. "Exactly."

CHAPTER TWENTY-NINE

"LET'S GO," Eric said. "One more stop."

Anika and I looked at each other. She was probably thinking the same thing I was: that I wanted to stay here forever.

"Unless you're too tired?" he said, a hint of goading in his voice.

Something in me fought against his words. Maybe the same part that wanted to prove my mom wrong, that got me up each morning to work out and kept me from eating unhealthy food.

"I'm game," I said.

Anika's watch lit up. "Yeah, me too. As long as we're back by midnight."

"You have a curfew?" I asked, teasing.

Eric smirked. "More like a booty call."

Anika's blush told me he wasn't far off.

"Kyle's taking me on a date when they get done watching film," she said.

My heart did something between melting and freezing. This was my first Friday night as a college student, and I was spending it with two people I barely knew, not my boyfriend, like Anika would be soon.

I got my phone out of my pocket again and checked the screen. Nothing.

"Let's go," I said.

We went back down the elevator and stepped onto the campus that looked so different now. Part of me longed to be back in the tower, seeing everything, but removed from it. Removed from my problems.

Life didn't work like that, though. The broken pieces had to be held together, even though they knew what it felt like to be shattered, separated.

"Where are we going?" Anika asked.

"You'll see, beautiful," Eric said.

Her lips pulled against her smile. "Uh huh."

I walked a little bit behind them, feeling out of place. But to be honest, it had been a while since I'd felt *in* place. Probably not since the chili cook-off when all of my friends and I were wearing those ridiculous shirts...

"Is she always this quiet?" Eric asked Anika.

Anika shrugged. "Kind of."

"I'm right here!" I protested.

Anika gave me a guilty smile. "You're just busy and tired, I think, from track."

Eric studied me a moment before looking back to the sidewalk in front of him. "Your parents must be really proud of you."

I wanted to ask what he saw that would make him think so, but not in front of Anika. So I just lied and said, "They are."

He stepped into the parking lot, stopping at a nice pickup parked in a staff spot.

"How did you get a spot this close?" I asked. "I practically need a map to find my car."

He shrugged. "Perks of working on the grounds crew."

I gave him a teasing smile. "There had to be one, right?"

"Ha ha," he said, opening the front and back doors on the passenger side. "Get in."

"You're bossy," I said.

"You're cute."

My cheeks heated, but I didn't reply to his comment. I just got in the back seat, leaving Anika the front. Sitting too close to him felt like a betrayal to Jon. If I was being honest, this whole night, enjoying myself, kind of felt that way.

He drove us about a mile away to a street lined with neon signs and people walking along the sidewalks. As we stepped out of the pickup, I realized most of them were our age.

"High Street," Eric said. "All the college kids hang out here."

Anika's eyes went wide. "Weed's not legal here though."

Eric shrugged. "Preemptive name?"

I took it all in, noticing the way some people staggered. How the girls wore even less clothing here than they did on campus. How the guys' eyes were constantly roaming. I looked down at my own outfit, running shorts and a T-shirt. My legs weren't even freshly shaven. Great. And how did all of these girls look so in shape and manage to have visible cleavage? I was on the track team and wouldn't feel comfortable wearing clothes like that.

Eric took my hand and squeezed. "You're gonna love this."

He let go almost immediately, but my stomach was still all over the place when we got to the front doors of a place called Big Hoss Tacos. The sign up front advertised "the biggest tacos in town."

I raised my eyebrows. We'd gone from the bell tower to *this*? The two places couldn't be more at odds with each other.

"Come on," he said, catching my look. "You have to get the full campus experience."

"What are we here for, then?" I asked. "The freshman fifteen?"

Anika pushed my arm. "Girl, please. You're on the track team. I'm sure you could use the calories."

That was the thing, though. I couldn't. I rubbed my arm. Like Nikki said, I needed to get my nutrition on point and work hard to deserve my spot on the team. Greasy red meat and full-fat sour cream didn't exactly fit into that plan.

"I'll have some guac," I decided before I even followed them through the doors.

I froze, though, right in the entryway. The last person I'd expected to see was directly in front of me, having the time of his life.

CHAPTER THIRTY

JON SAT in a booth only a few yards off, surrounded by guys I only recognized from the track team, and they had an entire platter of fatty Mexican food in front of them. There were a couple of girls there, too, squeezed in between the guys.

Jon was at the heart of it all, laughing, joking, smiling, living it up like there wasn't a message from me on his phone that he'd read hours before, wanting to make things right.

Anika followed my eyes, and with a smile, asked. "Isn't that Jon? We should go say hi."

But I wasn't smiling. I turned away and left the restaurant as fast as I could. I couldn't stand the sight, much less the odor, of that place. I didn't need corn and bean smells filling my nose, especially not now with my stomach turning and tears stinging my eyes.

I wiped at a few errant drops sliding down my cheeks. Why was I crying? It wasn't like I'd caught Jon with some leggy brunette sitting in his lap and feeding him chimichangas. I'd seen him doing exactly what he'd told me he'd be doing.

But there *were* girls there. If girlfriends were invited, why hadn't he asked me to come along? Anika and I could have been hanging out with him instead of some flirtatious rando I just met that week.

I spotted an empty bench outside a restaurant and fell onto it. My hands worked their way through my hair, which felt gritty since I still needed a shower. All of my insecurities rose up, bigger than ever before. I stared at the gum-speckled cement below me, trying to figure out how I'd gone from not believing in marriage to becoming one of those girls whose life revolved around a boy and a future with him.

I used to pick books from horror writers like Edgar Allen Poe and Steven King, just so I wouldn't have to read one more page about a heroine's life ending over rejection from a guy who couldn't care less. I'd had enough of that from my father. I didn't need to read it too.

But now?

No matter how much I hated it, Jon was my everything. In the span of months, he'd gone from someone I'd never even heard of to someone I couldn't live without. But what was I to him? From the way he was acting in the restaurant, I was nothing.

Someone sat next to me on the bench, and a small, silly, romantic part of me hoped it would be Jon. That he'd seen me in the restaurant, shoved everyone away to chase me, and come to sort things out. But this was real life. My life. The furthest thing from fantasy.

So I kept my eyes down, away. Maybe if I pretended whoever it was didn't exist, they wouldn't ask me questions. Wouldn't joke or make fun. After all, that sounded more realistic, and I'd had enough torment to fill my lifetime quota.

"So that's the guy you've been blowing me off for?" It wasn't the voice I'd been longing to hear. It was Eric's.

The guy I've been blowing him off for? More like my boyfriend, the guy who got me on the college track team and the man I'd been not-so-secretly planning the rest of my life with.

But instead of saying all of that, I just nodded, my head still in my hands.

He gently took my shoulders and peeled me up from the pathetic heap I was in. "Hey, you're too pretty to be sad."

I scoffed at him. "So ugly people deserve to be sad?" If so...

"Cut me some slack, smart aleck." He jokingly jostled my shoulders. "I'm not used to comforting girls I barely know over guys I'm jealous of."

I wasn't going there with a ten-foot pole. "I don't want to eat tacos," I said. At his snort, I added, "And don't even think of making a joke about girls eating tacos."

He lifted his hands. "Hey, you're the dirty-minded one who brought it up."

"Uh huh."

Anika came up to us, breathless. "What is going on? I turned around and you guys were gone!"

I pulled at the hem of my shorts. "I'm sorry."

"Don't be. What's going on between you two anyway?"

I wasn't sure whether she was asking about Eric and me or Jon and me. Either way, I said, "Nothing." Shaking my head, I stood up. "Come on, let's go back to the dorm."

Eric's eyes widened. "You want to leave?"

I gestured at my mess of a self. "I think it's *high* time."

There was barely a smirk on his face. "That's the best you can do?"

"Under the circumstances?" I shrugged. "Just being blunt."

That lightened the mood. A little. Jon was the first person I pun-warred with, and it just made me miss him more.

Eric drove us home, but there wasn't much conversation. Laying my guts bare in front of him felt wrong. So, once we got back, Anika asked the million-dollar question yet again. What was going on?

It was only fair to tell her, after running out of the restaurant on her, so I did. We sat on our beds, leaning back against opposite walls, and I spilled my taco-less guts. When I finished my story about feeling inadequate and Jon's comments from earlier, she shook her head.

"I know how you feel."

I raised my eyebrows. How could she possibly know how I felt? Anika was beautiful. And not in the way evil head cheerleaders in movies were beautiful. In the way that you knew would last until she was older with gray weaving its way through her hair. Together, she and Kyle looked like a couple from a perfume ad. All that was missing were a couple horses and a flower crown.

"Seriously." She bit her lip, looking over her shoulder, and when her eyes met mine again, they were full of pain. "My first boyfriend. He told me he loved me, all the things you want to hear from a guy." She rolled her eyes, fluttering her lids quickly against the moisture appearing there. Her voice turned bitter. "And then once he got what he wanted, he left. Sent me a text saying he didn't see me as more than a friend."

My mouth fell open, unable to find the words for how horrible that must have been.

"Jon loves you," she said. "Kyle told me he talks about you all the time."

I cringed, running my fingers through the end of my ponytail. "Then why does it feel this way?" Why wouldn't he reply to my message if communicating was what relationships were all about?

"Maybe because you won't let yourself believe you're good enough for that kind of love. So you're always worrying about when it's going to end instead of enjoying what you have."

Her words hit me like a punch to the oversized

gut. If there were a magical button I could flip to love myself, I would, in a heartbeat. I'd dieted, lost weight, worked hard, started college. By everyone else's standards, even the national statistics about kids with abusive, drug addict parents, I'd made it. So why didn't it feel that way?

Anika gave me a knowing smile with sadness in her eyes. "It just takes time," she said. "One day, you wake up, and you realize that the people who love you—even when you can't love yourself—those are the people whose opinions matter."

"But how do you get from here to there?" I asked, desperate.

"This is how I started," she said. "When someone shows you they love you, listen."

I fell asleep that night thinking about Anika's words. When I woke in the morning, my phone showed new words from Jon.

CHAPTER THIRTY-ONE

A KNOCK SOUNDED on the door at eleven in the morning. Jon was here right on time, just like he'd promised in his text message. But that was all he had promised.

I'd already gone on a two-mile run to keep my muscles working, eaten an egg white omelet, nuts, and fruits for breakfast, and knocked out homework for two of my classes. None of that had eased the tightness in my chest though.

No, only opening the door and seeing Jon there, holding two coffees and smiling at me with his bright green eyes did that.

Love. That's what that was.

I took both the drinks from his hands, put them on my desk, and launched into his arms.

His chest lifted and fell with a slow breath. He'd needed this too. I fisted the T-shirt at his back and leaned into his shoulder, breathing it all in. His cologne, the laundry detergent he'd brought from home, the sweet ease and preciousness of every moment I had in his arms, just like this.

Why did we make it so complicated when just *being* together felt so good?

Jon pulled back and kissed the top of my head. "It's good to see you too."

I returned his smile and echoed my text from the night before. "I'm ready to talk when you are."

"Good," he said. "But first." He reached around me and picked up the coffees. "I thought we could check out the library."

My stomach twisted with guilt. I'd seen the entire campus, the dark corners of the library last night without him. But everything was new when I was with Jon.

"I'm game," I said.

I followed him out of the room and locked the door behind me. We walked across campus together, sipping slowly from our drinks, even though it was still hot outside.

"What did you end up doing last night?" he asked.

I could tell he hadn't seen me at Big Hoss Tacos from the way he asked, so I left my meltdown out of the conversation. "Anika and I went out with someone from class. Walked around campus, checked out High Street."

He seemed surprised. "I didn't see you."

"Oh?" But I saw you. I still had the pain in my chest to prove it.

"Yeah, I went with some of the guys to get dinner after we studied," he said. "A few of them brought their girlfriends. I wish I would have known."

"That's alright," I said. I wasn't jealous of the girlfriends. I was jealous of Jon. Of the casual way he said "some of the guys." He was already at home in this new place, and I was still so lost. Heck, I'd felt more at home with my parents than I did here. What kind of sadistic person was I to feel so comfortable in pain that I didn't know how to live in normalcy?

"You're quiet," he said.

I scuffed my toe on the sidewalk and looked up at him. "I know. I'm trying to work on that." My voice cracked. "I don't want to ruin this."

"Abi." Even though people were all around us, he stopped and put his hands on my shoulders, holding his coffee between his thumb and index finger. When I wouldn't meet his eyes, he dipped down and caught my gaze with his own. "Abi."

"Yes?" I asked, my voice thick.

"I want this, you and me, so much." His words struck me in the core, and whatever hope I had left clung to every single one. "I just don't want you to shut me out."

"I don't want to," I said. "What do you want to know?"

"Everything." He took my hand and changed direction, away from the library.

He stopped at a patch of grass away from the sidewalk, away from everyone, and got comfortable, laying on the ground. His arms were open, inviting. "Lie with me?"

I did, resting my head on his chest. With the beat of his heart in one ear and the sun warming my skin, I was melting from the inside out.

"Tell me about classes," he prompted.

I started with communications, about the teacher who made snarky comments about people walking in late, but I couldn't bring myself to mention Eric. I didn't want to worry Jon over nothing. And then I talked about taking the ice bath with the girls and how I actually had a few people I knew on the track team. Maybe I wasn't as far from finding home as I had thought.

"What happened with the nutritionist?" he asked, and I got the feeling he'd been waiting all along just for this one question.

I sighed and sat up, suddenly feeling itchy where the grass had touched my skin.

He propped himself up too. "What?" he asked.

"She's an idiot," I snapped. "How she managed to get a job as a nutritionist for a division one program, I have no idea."

"It was that bad?" he asked. "Everything she told me seemed pretty standard. You know, fruits, vegetables, lean protein—what's the deal?"

Of course Jon got the sweet version of *Deborah*. He was destined to be the golden boy, and I was the girl who could never be good enough, no matter how hard I tried.

"She told me I needed to bulk up."

"What?" he scoffed. "That doesn't make any sense."

Part of me was hurt he immediately balked at me needing to gain weight. Like he could have told me I was slim and would look good with some more "meat on my bones." But he was right. It was ridiculous.

"I'm a distance runner," I said. "I don't need to be carrying around extra weight."

"Especially when you've worked so hard to get to this point," he said.

A burden the size of Texas lifted from my shoulders to have Jon on my team again. To know he recognized how hard I'd been working. It was all for him and our future.

"I just don't know what to do," I said. "I want to keep getting better."

"Maybe talk to your coach?" he suggested. "Or make an appointment with a nutritionist outside of the college. There's nothing wrong with a second opinion."

I leaned back into his arms and hugged him. "I love you."

"I love you too." His palms slid up my arms to my shoulders. "Now, how about we kiss and make up?"

"That's the best idea I've heard all day." I pressed my lips to his, tender, sweet, warm. His mouth parted, welcoming me in. Showing me that home had a flavor, and this was it. His hands worked up my back, gripped the hair at the base of my neck, sent shivers through my entire body until my breath came quick and my pulse came quicker.

When Jon pulled back, his lids were heavy, his

eyes hazy as they landed on my mouth. "Let's get out of here?" he asked.

"I like that idea even better."

We spent the afternoon together doing exactly what I'd dreamed college would be like. Spending time with Jon. Exploring campus. Exploring each other and this crazy thing called love.

After a day of bliss, I went back to my dorm room and saw the only thing that could bring me right back to reality. A plain envelope and clear block lettering someone had slid under my door.

CHAPTER THIRTY-TWO

You made up? How long do you think it will last?

FEAR FLOODED MY BODY, making it feel like someone was there. Watching me. I ran to the door and made sure it was locked, then checked our windows, even though we were on the tenth floor. No one was getting in here.

But that didn't keep me from checking underneath our beds, in the closets. Desperate tears clung to my lashes. I couldn't live like this. Couldn't be digging through my dorm room looking for a threat that may or may not exist.

And I definitely couldn't do it alone.

So, I called the one person who had been there for me, no matter what.

She picked up after only two rings, and a smile shone in her voice. "Hi, sweetheart."

Just Grandma's greeting was enough to make tears prick at my eyes. "Grandma. I miss you."

"Oh, honey. You know I'm always a phone call away." Her words were a hug, healing and ripping. Reminding me of everything I missed from home.

I sniffed, seconds from losing it all. "I know." My voice came out small.

"What do you need?" she asked. "How can I help?"

"Can't you just tell me what I need like usual?" I half laughed, half cried.

She laughed too. "You're an adult, sweetie. And you have been for a while. It's about time I started treating you that way."

I had no words. Not a single one.

"Let's hear it," she said.

"I'm still getting those letters," I told her. "Like what I got at graduation."

The line was quiet for a moment. "You didn't figure out who was doing it?"

"No," I said. My voice got small. "I'm starting to get worried, Gram."

"Have you called the police?"

I shook my head, then realized she couldn't see me. "No, I haven't."

"I would do that first," she suggested. "Bring them the notes."

Just the thought of going to the police station felt like jumping into the ice bath headfirst. "The last time I was around police..." I cringed, remembering the visit to the prison. And them questioning me about my parents' drug use before that.

"Oh." She paused. "Do you want me to call them?"

My voice was small as I said, "Yes."

"Tell me what the letters said."

I got them out of my drawer and read them all aloud. None of them said anything real or threatening, if you didn't have the context.

"If this is a joke, it isn't a funny one," she said. "Do they have a return address?"

"No."

"Do you have any idea who it could be?"

"None." I'd thought of this a million and one times. "I mean, my parents are in prison. I don't really know anyone else who would want to hurt me."

"I'll call you right back."

The line went silent, and my eyes went wide.

Grandma was calling the police. I gripped my cell phone in both hands and went to the window to wait while Grandma talked to them. We had a great view of the parking lot. Of the tiny cars pulling in and leaving, driving in circles looking for a spot that wasn't a day's hike away. Some people walked out there, carrying massive hampers of laundry.

I wondered if their lives were as normal as they looked or if they were like me. Could they be like me?

My phone rang, and I was in such a rush to answer it, it fell to the floor, sliding underneath my dresser.

I got on my hands and knees—learned we needed to sweep and mop—and retrieved it. I swiped the answer button and held it to my ear, still lying on my stomach. "Hello?"

"Bad news," Grandma said.

My heart fell. "What?"

"They said if you don't know who it is, there isn't much they can do. If you did find out, you could file a victim protective order, but other than that..."

"I'm on my own."

"You are not," she said. "You have me. And Jon."

I smiled at the thought. "I haven't told Jon yet. I

don't want to worry them if there's nothing we can do."

"Abi, I—"

"Please, Gram?" I asked. "Don't tell them. There's already enough drama in my life. I don't need their worry too."

Begrudgingly, she said yes, but then added, "But I still think you should tell Jon. He's been through a lot, too. He's stronger than you think."

I didn't doubt how strong he was. He just deserved better.

"So what are you going to do?" she asked.

"What should I do?" I asked. "I'm terrified."

"This person is clearly a coward," Grandma said. "Whoever it is won't hurt you in front of other people. But just in case, I would head to the gun store and—"

"Grandma! I can't get a gun. I wouldn't even know the first—"

"Not to get a gun!" she cried. "They have other self-defense items. Pepper spray, tasers. Talk to an associate and have them set you up. Get whatever you need to feel safe and put it on the emergency credit card."

The stress of it all leaked out my eyes. "You mean it?"

"I let you stay in an unsafe situation before. I'm *never* making that mistake again."

All those years when I'd hidden in my room, abused by my parents without anyone who seemed to care...they washed away. Grandma cared; I could feel it in my core.

"I'm going now," I said.

"Good girl. Call me if you need anything at all."

I promised her I would and then hung up. The note sat on my desk like a flashing neon sign reminding me that no matter how far away I got from my parents, I'd never escape fearing for my safety. For my life.

I balled up the note and threw it in the trash, anger replacing disbelief. Sure, I wanted to know who was sending these and how they seemed to know so much about my life. But really, I wanted to punch them in the throat for ruining this moment for me.

Didn't I have enough on my plate? Didn't I have enough worries? I wasn't going to let whoever this was take my focus off what was important to me: Jon and continuing to prove I was good enough to be here—with him.

When I lived with my parents, I was defenseless. I had no money, but that wasn't the case anymore.

Grandma had equipped me with a credit card and told me to spend as much as I needed to feel safe.

I left my dorm, looking over my shoulder every few seconds to make sure I wasn't followed, and went straight to the gun store.

I walked inside, greeted by stuffed animals with huge horns and glassy eyes. In the back, rifles lined the walls, just like the ones we'd seen in the back windows of vehicles at the chili cook-off.

I wondered what it would feel like to grip the smooth wood. To know that what I held in my hands was stronger, more powerful, than any person.

More powerful than me.

"Can I help you?" an older man dressed in the store colors asked, looking down his nose at me.

"I have a stalker," I said, my voice sounding strange, even to me. "The cops can't do anything, and I need to defend myself."

A corner of his lips lifted. "We've got you covered."

The sales associate set me up with a stun gun and pepper spray, along with a keychain he swore could be lethal, a pointed ring I was supposed to wear at all times, an alarm button, and even a pocketknife.

Before I left the store, he made sure I had the

items connected to my keychain, in an accessible spot, and my ring slipped on my finger.

"These won't do you any good if you're not ready," he said.

The words doused my self-defense flames with ice water. This wasn't the type of thing I could shop away. I needed to be ready, whenever, wherever.

CHAPTER THIRTY-THREE

ON MONDAY MORNING, I slid into my seat next to Eric in communications with seconds to spare before the bell. He had just enough time to run his fingers through his wavy hair and smile at me before Prof Warren started talking about the upcoming week.

"Group project, with an oral presentation, due Friday. On Monday, we'll have a test over the presentations. Attendance is mandatory," she said and began passing massive packets of paper down each row. "Look at the person beside you. I hope you like them, because they're your partner for the rest of the semester."

Eric sent me another grin, and my stomach made an uneasy turn. I didn't want to have any more of an excuse to talk to him or cross lines that should be drawn in more than just sand.

I looked at the instructions on the handout. Each group had to take a section from the book and present on it. My mouth fell open. "She's having us teach the class."

His shoulders lifted in a shrug. "Welcome to college."

Before the bell rang, we made a plan to meet in the dining hall during his lunch break for the rest of the week to work on the assignment. I wasn't crazy about giving up the one hour a day I had with Jon, but it was the only time we had that didn't interfere with his work schedule or my track practices.

When I made it to my next class a few minutes early, I settled into an empty seat near the back where I'd at least have some privacy. I got out my phone and sent Jon a text to break the bad news.

Abi: Group assignments are the worst. :(My partner can only meet at lunchtime this week.

Jon: Ugh. That stinks.

Jon: I could use the extra study time. Cumulative, essay answer exam in philosophy.

Abi: Essay answer?

Jon: By hand.

Abi: Yuck.

Jon: I know. I'm more sad I won't get to see you.

My heart melted at his words.

Abi: We'll have this weekend, though, right?

Jon: Of course. I'm not letting you out of my sight.

Abi: Good.

The professor began talking, quieting the students. I glanced up at the front of the room, where the professor had a slide on the screen with the headline TEST REVIEW.

I swore under my breath.

Abi: Gotta go. Just got assigned a test.

Jon: Good luck, beautiful.

Abi: I'll need it.

I shoved my phone in my pocket and listened to blow after blow.

Cumulative exam.

Short answer.

Friday.

My other two classes only brought more bad news.

Tests. Tests. And more tests.

Had all of my teachers gotten together and decided we should all have exams before the long Labor Day weekend? Because they piled on the assignments like they had. And apparently, Jon's had too. Judging by our homework piles and impending exam dates, the first two weeks of college had been a joke compared to what now amounted to an entire mountain of homework assignments and group projects.

And since the boys' and girls' track teams had settled into what Coach Cadence said was the regular schedule, Jon and I wouldn't even get to walk to practice together anymore. If my weights were in the morning, his were in the evening. If Coach Cadence planned a long run for the evening, Jon was up before the sun for his.

As I walked to the dining hall an hour later than normal to meet with Eric—not Jon—it struck me how much I preemptively missed him. I never knew I could be so homesick for a person who only lived a floor away from me, but my entire body seemed to drag with the feeling.

Eric looked up from his phone and gave me a smile.

I dropped into my chair, setting my tray on the table a little harder than necessary.

"Long day?" he asked.

"Yep. And it's only noon. Let's get started?"

His hand reached across the table and grabbed mine. "What's this?"

I glanced down at the promise ring on my finger.

Just seeing it warmed my heart. "My boyfriend gave that to me."

"No." His thumb ran over the sharp tips of my self-defense ring.

"Nothing," I said, pulling my hand back and coming up with a lie. "My grandma's super paranoid about me being away at college, so she had me get a few things."

He chuckled. "Protective grandma, huh? What all did she have you get?"

I tried to make light of it as I listed the things I had—from pepper spray to the stun gun.

"Well," he said, "you can never be too safe. You never know when someone out there wants to cause you harm."

His eyes darkened, and I wanted to ask the story behind his expression, but something told me it was a secret he held close to his heart.

"Let's get started?" I suggested.

He nodded.

After our study session, I walked back to the dorm to settle in for some studying before track practice. When I went to turn the door handle, it was unlocked.

My heart leapt to my throat, pounding harder

than it had in every race, while I stood frozen, trying to decide my next steps.

Did I go in? Would someone be there?

"Anika?" I called.

She didn't answer.

"Anika?" I yelled, louder this time.

When she still didn't answer, I glanced back and forth down the hallway. Empty.

I firmed my hand on the pepper spray on my keychain, twisted the handle, and kicked the door open. It swung back, too heavy to bang against the opposite wall.

At first glance, there was no one in the room.

I stepped inside, still wielding my pepper spray. Anika was nowhere to be seen.

But neither was anyone else.

I went through my routine, checking under the beds, in the closets, in the space beneath the desks.

My heart was still racing when I locked the door behind me and sat in my desk chair. How had Anika been so careless to leave the room unlocked? I always locked it when I left.

I got out my phone and sent Anika a text message. Or three.

Abi: You left the door unlocked.

Abi: I was terrified.

Abi: Haven't you heard of all the things that have happened to girls in dorm buildings?

Abi: Our stuff could have been stolen.

My fingers flew over my keyboard as I pounded out each message.

Anika: Whoa. I'm sorry, okay?

Her cavalier response just made me more angry. This wasn't a simple mistake to me. It was life or death. But she didn't know that, which was my fault. I took a deep breath and let it loose through flared nostrils.

Abi: Just be more careful next time.

She didn't reply, which was probably for the best.

I couldn't focus on my homework, so I just lay in my bed, feeling the hum of adrenaline slowly leave my body as the sales associates words echoed through my mind.

They won't do any good if you're not ready.

But how could you ever be ready for something you couldn't see?

CHAPTER THIRTY-FOUR

AFTER THE LATEST TORTURE-TRAINING RUN, Nikki, Mollie, Jayne, and I showered in the locker room and then went to the dining hall together. While they loaded their trays with full-fat food, I had to pick only the healthiest foods from the salad bar. As I dabbed grease from my grilled chicken, I eyed their plates with envy. How could they eat hamburgers and salads drenched in ranch when I had to eat like this just to avoid ballooning?

But then I remembered. I'd done this to myself with years of overeating. Really, my parents had done this to me. But it was up to me to fix it.

"We should go dancing tonight," Nikki said.

Mollie eyed her. "Are you crazy? We just ran ten miles."

Jayne shrugged. "It could be fun."

Nikki nodded. "You in, Abi?"

I eyed my barely touched food. If it got my mind off Jon and how absolutely long this week would be without him, it would be worth it. "I'm game."

"Good." She shoved the rest of her burger in her mouth and talked through the food. "Go get dressed, girls. I'll meet you downstairs in ten."

As I walked to my dorm, I sent Jon a quick text. More out of hope than anything. He'd been too tired or busy to talk the last couple nights.

Abi: Going out with some friends. Might not have my phone. Can we talk?

Jon: I'd like that.

Within a few minutes, my phone rang, his name on the screen. His voice in my ear was better than anything I'd tasted all day. I let out a breath, feeling lighter already.

"I miss you," I said.

"I miss you too." His voice was full of honesty...and regret?

"What's going on?" I asked.

"I can't go to Woodman for Labor Day," he said. "One of my dad's cousins is in the hospital in Amarillo. I think he needs me there."

I should have been sad, worried, offered help,

but my first thought was that Jon wouldn't be spending Labor Day weekend with me. And who knew the next time we'd get a full weekend together?

Then I realized what a terrible person that made me and felt even worse. "I'm sorry." I apologized for my thoughts, even though he hadn't heard them. "Will she...he? be okay?"

"I'm not sure," he said. "She just passed out at work, and they don't know what's going on."

"That's awful. Are she and your dad close?"

"Like siblings. My dad isn't taking it well." The inflection in his voice was clear. While I'd been thinking of myself, he'd been worried about his dad. That was one of the reasons I loved Jon. He always cared for others before himself.

"I can come with you," I said. "Grandma and Stormy will understand."

"No," he replied, too fast. "You have a good time. Both of our weekends shouldn't be ruined."

I didn't tell him that not seeing him, not being there to support him, would ruin my weekend. Instead, I played the good girlfriend I knew I should. "Okay, let me know if I can do anything."

"Have fun tonight," he offered. "You can do that for me."

"What?" I reached my dorm and put my key in the door. It was locked this time.

"With your friends? Aren't you going out?"

"Yeah, I am." How had I already forgotten about that? Jon had my heart, mind, soul. I needed to focus, though. "Some girls from the track team are going dancing."

"You should bring Anika," he said. "Kyle said she's lonely."

I felt guilty enough already for going off on her for what was probably an innocent mistake. I knew just as well as her that no one locked anything in Roderdale.

I spotted her at her desk, bent over a textbook, and said a simple "I will" to Jon so as to not give anything away.

"Okay, I gotta run," he said and rushed out a hurried, "Love you."

I barely had enough time to say it back before he'd hung up the phone.

Anika looked up. "Jon's still busy?"

She seemed to be ignoring the locked-door debacle. I would too. I liked that plan.

"Yeah." I turned into my closet to hide my stinging eyes. I knew how pathetic it was that I was this upset simply because I couldn't spend a weekend without him. "Some girls from the track team are going dancing tonight. Wanna come?"

"I wish." She huffed. "If you see my psych professor while you're out, can you trip her or something?"

"Trip her?" I laughed. "That's the best you can do?"

"Spike her drink?"

"While she's out drinking?" I teased. "Want me to tickle her with a feather while I'm at it?"

Anika buried her face even farther in her textbook, giggling. "I'm bad at this!"

"That's okay." I laughed. "Just means you're nice." And don't have two terrible parents you used to plot revenge against. "I'll catch you tomorrow?"

"Yeah."

I threw a blouse over my head and some jeans.

"Hey," Anika said. "I got the mail. Yours is on your desk."

"Thanks." I eyed the envelope without a return address. Then I walked out the door.

CHAPTER THIRTY-FIVE

THIS TIME, Mollie drove. She had a car with a backseat so we didn't have to get all wind-whipped on the way to High Street. There was a glittery, zebra-striped flask of rum in the center console that we all shared. (Except for Mollie. Because she was driving, and we weren't idiots.)

How much Captain Morgan does it take to get three girls on the track team tipsy, you ask?

It was less than one flask.

Everything about me was already warm by the time Mollie found a parking spot by Big Hoss Tacos.

My stomach growled, and Nikki patted it, bending over so her face was level with my navel. "Wanna eat a taco, little guy?"

Mollie reached over and literally grabbed my

stomach flab, pushing it together and grumbled. "Feed me. Abi hungry."

I swatted her hand away and covered my middle. "Don't grab my fat!"

Jayne rolled her eyes. "What fat?"

I narrowed my gaze. "You don't have to be nice *all* the time."

"Whatever," Nikki said, "come on. We gotta show Abi Freddie Mash."

"What?" There was something funny about that name, but I couldn't peg what it was with my mind all fuzzy and my stomach still warm.

Nikki looped her arm through mine, her bracelet scratching across my skin. "It's a dance bar we can actually get into."

"Oh." My eyes landed on her midsection.

While I'd gone simple with a blouse and jeans, she'd gone all out with a revealing top that showed off every line of her muscled stomach.

Jealousy ached through me. I'd die before showing off all of my lines. They weren't the good ones. They were the kind that got red when I sat down for too long because my skin folded over against itself. Not sexy.

Now that I looked at our group walking, it was clear how out of place I was. Mollie had dressed just as scantily with a tank top that tied in the back with thin spaghetti straps. Even Jayne sported a short denim dress fraying at the edges.

Their outfits—and fitness—made me miss my friends that much more. I had a feeling these girls wouldn't be partaking in the saltine challenge.

We reached the dingy Freddie Mash building, indicated by a big neon sign. The S in Mash was a flashing dollar sign. A big guy at the door wrote big dollar signs on each of our hands in permanent marker.

Nikki looped her arm over my shoulders and whispered loudly, "Don't worry. We'll wash it off in the bathroom."

Even on a Wednesday night, the place was packed with dancing, drinking bodies. I almost collided with a glass full of amber liquid and basically did the limbo to miss it.

"Go, Abi!" Mollie cheered.

Nikki laughed, and then I did too. Because everything was funnier when I felt like this.

We went to the bathroom, and Mollie got hand sanitizer out of her purse. We all got our dollar signs off, drained the rest of the flask, and went back into the bar with all the confidence of freshly non-underage bar-goers.

Which wasn't much. I might as well have had a flashing neon sign over my head that said RULE BREAKER for how guilty I felt.

There was a pause between songs, and one of the guys lining the dancefloor quickly grabbed Nikki. I watched in awe as she spun with him onto the hardwood, her pointed boots flashing so quickly the pair had to have practiced before now.

Some guy in a cowboy hat grabbed Mollie next, and then one of his friends asked Jayne to dance.

She gave me a questioning look before I nodded, and she was led into the throng of people.

No one asked me to dance. It felt kind of like being picked last for the dodgeball team. And then getting hit the face with the ball over and over again.

Plus, I was only a few miles from the dorm, but I might as well have been on Mars for how alien I felt. Where had all these people in boots and cowboy hats come from? We were in Austin for crying out loud. The last cow I'd seen was at least half an hour away at Nikki's house.

I wrapped my arms around my waist and wished for a drink just for something to do with my hands if nothing else.

Then I remembered my phone. The perfect

distraction. I loved it even more now than I did when I got it for Christmas.

I pulled it out and snapped a quick picture before sending it to Stormy.

Abi: HELP

Stormy: You're at a bar???!

Abi: More like on the moon.

Abi: One small step for man, one giant step backward for womankind.

Stormy: LOL girl, I'm so jealous.

Stormy: Frankie just dared me to cut his toenails.

Abi: sTOP

Stormy sent me a photo of hairy toes with excruciatingly long toenails. Well, except for the big toenail, which was a semi-decent length.

Abi: I just threw up.

Stormy: Been drinking?

Abi: NO. FROM THAT MONSTROSITY YOUR MAN CALLS A FOOT.

Stormy: It's not that bad.

Abi: Did he at least shower before this?

Stormy: It doesn't smell that bad.

Abi: You keep saying "that bad" like that makes it any better.

"What are you smiling about?" a low voice hummed.

I glanced over and groaned out loud. "How are you *everywhere*? Are you stalking me?"

Eric chuckled and shrugged. "Went out with some guys." He nodded toward a group sitting in one of the booths edging the bar. They were still wearing their Upton grounds crew uniforms. "Saw you standing here by yourself. Don't tell me you came here looking for love."

"For your information," I said, "I've already found it."

He smirked. "Yes, you have."

I rolled my eyes, but before I could tell him he was wrong, he had my hand in his and was tugging me toward the throng of people.

"No, no, no, no, no," I said, stuttering my feet on the ground. "I cannot dance."

"You can't," he said, "but I can." He spun me, and before I could lose my phone, I shoved it in my back pocket.

Right in time too, because he'd pulled me close to him, and all I could do was hold on. His breath poured over my face, smelling tangy like beer.

Jon's breath never smelled like beer.

I stepped on his toe, and he pretended to be hurt.

"I don't feel sorry for you at all," I yelled over the music. I had to be right next to his ear for him to hear me. Close enough to see the sweat beading on his forehead and to smell the cologne on his shirt. "I told you I can't dance."

"Fast, fast, slow, fast, fast, slow," he said in response, trying to show me the steps.

It was hopeless. Jon and I weren't two-steppers. We were hopping-in-place-ers.

Thank God a fast song saved me. I didn't know how much longer I could keep dancing with this guy who wasn't Jon.

I started to leave the dance floor, but Eric grabbed my arm. "Where do you think you're going?"

CHAPTER THIRTY-SIX

I LOOKED from his hand on my arm to the toying smile on his face. Why it unsettled me, I didn't know.

I leaned closer and yelled, "Bathroom."

"Ah." He nodded and released me.

As quickly as I could, I made it through shifting bodies to the bathroom and locked myself in a stall. This wasn't nearly as peaceful as I'd come to expect from metal stalls, though.

Instead, I was surrounded by graphic writing and doodles on the walls, and I could hear someone throwing up a few stalls over. A couple of girls giggling. Plus, the entire floor was permanently wet and dotted with moist toilet paper.

Still, I covered the toilet seat in tissue and gave myself a rest. I needed it.

Really, I needed Jon. I missed him. He should have been here with me, dancing, having a good time, saving me from guys—whether it was a lack of attention or too much.

I sent him a bathroom selfie, a goofy photo of me sitting on the stall.

Jon: God I miss you.

Abi: I miss you too. Come out?

Jon: Too much homework :(

Abi: I can come there?

Jon: Then I really won't get anything done.

My heart sank. The logic side of my brain knew homework was important. Our education was the whole reason we were here. But the emotional idiot inside of me wanted to scream and cry.

Jon: I'm thinking of you. Every second.

But why did that make my chest hurt more?

I wiped a tear from my eye and replied.

Abi: When is it going to be better?

I read Jon's three-word reply, and a wave of hopelessness washed over me.

Jon: I don't know.

Breathing in deeply—and then instantly regretting it because I was in a disgusting bar bathroom—I stood up and went to the sinks. I stared into the mirror, watching the way my hair hung lank around my face, sagging from sweat and heat and humidity. The way the dark circles under my eyes had grown so large and shadowed, I almost looked hollow.

Maybe I *was* hollow.

Who was I without Jon? Who was I without the gold holding my cracks together?

Here, in this bar, the last girl picked to dance, the gold seemed farther away than ever.

I sighed and walked out of the room, hoping this night was closer to the ending than it was to the beginning.

My eyes immediately went to the table where Eric's friends sat, and I was strangely relieved to see him sitting with them. Then I caught sight of my friends on the dance floor, all together having a good time.

It struck me that they were friends before I came along. I was the extra.

I wanted to call Jon, Grandma, someone, but I couldn't. Grandma would have just finished watching the ten o'clock news by now and would be getting ready for bed, and Jon, well, he already said he was preoccupied.

My mind latched onto the last person who had made me feel wanted, needed, and I dialed his number.

The rings repeated for so long, I almost hung up. But then his voice flooded the line.

"Hello?" Evan answered.

"Hey," I breathed, then said it again louder because there was no way he'd heard me over the music. "Hey! I'm going outside. Hold on!"

I looked over my shoulder to check the girls weren't looking for me, but they were lost in the music, in the crowd, in the *fun.*

I was just lost.

I stepped outside, and my ears hummed from being exposed to the noise for so long. As I walked farther down the sidewalk, my feet hurt. I missed my tennis shoes, my room, the quiet, no-questions-asked companionship Anika offered.

I turned the corner and leaned my back against the brick wall. Carefully, I shimmied down until I was sitting alongside the building, away from the main sidewalk.

"Hey," I said, finally.

"Hey," Evan repeated. "What's up?"

I rolled my glassy eyes toward the sky but only saw black and streetlights. "Oh, you know." My voice cracked. "Just having the time of my life."

"Are you okay?"

"What does that even mean?" I asked.

"I—I don't know. Do you need me to call some-one, come there?"

"No." I sniffed and rubbed my arm over my face for good measure. "No, I'm fine. How's JuCo?"

"Like winning a Grammy while holding an Oscar," he said with a sarcastic tone. "How's being a D1 athlete slash badass?"

I laughed. Just the gesture seemed rough. Like I was out of practice. "I'm exhausted," I managed. "Trying to do some extra workouts to make up for where I started."

"Always going the extra mile." He chuckled. "Ha ha. Get it? Extra mile? Because you're a distance runner?" He forced a laugh again, clearly putting on a happy show for me.

Thank God for Evan. The smile that touched my lips was genuine. As was the exasperated eye-roll. "Your terrible jokes have reached the finish line."

He laughed again. "So, it's been rough? Where's Jon?" he added, almost as an afterthought.

"You have no idea," I said with a little more poise this time. "It's just..." What was it, though? "I can't believe I'm saying this, but I miss high school."

"I do too," he admitted. "Why did everyone act like college was going to be this amazing non-stop party?"

"Right?"

"Right. I mean, I've been here for three weeks, and I've had four tests, tons of homework, have made...maybe one friend, and my girlfriend is an hour away. Without her driver's license or a car."

"Well," I said, "that's kind of your fault for dating jailbait."

He laughed. "I resent that."

"Resent away."

"I miss you, Abi," he said. "We need to hang out when you're back, just us, okay?"

I touched the golden A that hung around my neck, remembering the last time we spent time alone. "Will Michele be okay with that?"

"I don't know," he said. "But she should be if she isn't."

My lips quirked. "Thanks, Evan. You always make things better."

"Thanks," he said. "But you don't need me to make things better. You're good at doing that all on your own. Look how far you've come since you moved to Woodman."

The warmth spreading through my heart was interrupted by a text message from Nikki.

Nikki: Where are you? Leaving in a few.

I pressed my phone back to my ear. "Thanks, Evan. I'll talk to you soon?"

"Any time. I'm just a phone call away."

CHAPTER THIRTY-SEVEN

TALKING TO EVAN WAS GREAT. Riding home with the girls was fun. But walking to my dorm, constantly looking over my shoulder and knowing I wouldn't see Jon tonight, o the next night, or this weekend, was torture.

I entered the room, ready to vent to Anika, but she was gone with a note on her desk.

At the library, cramming. Looks like it'll be an all-nighter. See you in the AM.

I held the index card between my fingers. I wouldn't call Anika and me close—not yet at least—but I missed her already.

It was late, though. I needed to get into bed, catch up on some of the sleep I'd been missing.

I texted Jon. If I couldn't have him here, I wanted

his name on my phone to be the last thing I saw before I went to sleep.

Abi: I miss you.

He didn't reply for several minutes, but finally, my phone vibrated.

Jon: I miss you too.

Abi: Come see me? Just for a minute?

I wasn't planning on asking, but my heart hurt in ways I didn't understand. Maybe it was more than just missing him. I did—miss him—but maybe it was missing how I dreamed college could be.

Jon: Can't. I need to get this assignment turned in by midnight.

Abi: After?

Jon: I have practice at 4:30. I'm beat. You understand, right?

My head did. My heart on the other hand... I texted back the only logical answer.

Abi: Of course.

Jon: Someday, we'll be able to fall asleep together every night. This will feel like nothing.

For feeling so low only moments ago, my heart soared.

Abi: You mean it?

Jon didn't reply, not for ten minutes, and not for

thirty. My stupid heart went right back plummeting to sub sea-level lows.

I tossed my phone on the canvas chair by my bed and tried to fall asleep. It was useless. An ache took physical space in my heart, in my mind, refusing to move. How could Jon's absence feel so *present*?

Around two in the morning, a few knocks sounded on my door, and I pushed myself out of bed. Anika probably forgot her keys.

It didn't matter that she'd gotten me up so late. I wasn't even close to going to sleep anyway.

But when I opened the door, Jon stood there, a dream in sweatpants and a track team T-shirt with messy hair.

"Jon, what are you..."

He drew me in and kissed me on my lips, silencing me. As he walked to my bed, holding my hand, he said, "I wanted to give you a taste of forever."

We lay curled on my twin mattress, our bodies pressed together, spreading warmth from every surface.

When I woke up, Jon was gone, but his smell, his memory was still there. If this was what forever felt like, I had to have it.

CHAPTER THIRTY-EIGHT

ON MY WALK TO lunch the next day, I was still thinking of Jon sleeping next to me all night. The fresh memory had revived every single butterfly in my stomach that had taken flight since the day I met him.

Something about sleeping next to him, on our own, made our relationship feel that much more real. More permanent.

And I realized I wanted more with him than what we had. I wanted everything.

I got my phone out, my fingers hovering over the list of contacts. I couldn't call Stormy because she wouldn't see what the big deal was. Or Skye, after the whole community shower comment—I would be too embarrassed, thinking of that the whole time. Or Macy and Leanne for...obvious reasons.

So I did the unthinkable. I called my grandma.

"Abi." Her voice sounded worried. "Is everything okay?"

"Yeah, yes," I said. "I just wanted to talk."

She let out a relieved breath. "I've been trying not to smother you, but..."

"I know," I said. I was touched at how much she cared. "Thank you."

"So what did you want to talk about?"

Even though I knew this was the right move, I stalled. What if she told Marta, and Marta got back to Jon, and then I'd look like a child running to my grandma for help?

"What is it?" Grandma asked.

Was I really going to have the sex talk with Grandma? "Um..." My cheeks flushed just thinking of it. Maybe we should just stick to stalker letters and defense mechanisms and call it a day.

"Just spit it out already."

There was my grandma. "Well, you know, sex?"

"Is that a question?"

I buried my face in my hands and groaned. No one passing around me on the sidewalk could hear what Grandma was saying—or cared—but still.

"You're having sex right now?" she cried.

"No!" I yelled, sputtering. "No, no no, no no way! Not yet, at least."

I could *feel* her sigh of relief across the phone. "So, Marta's abstinence comments didn't stick?" She chuckled.

"Okay, can I take it back? Let's talk about the cafeteria food."

She laughed again. "Honey, I'm going to tell you three things about sex, and if you have any more questions, well, I'm going to need some time to deal."

"Okay?"

"Okay." She drew a loud inhale and exhaled slowly. "Number one. Sex can be many things. Basic, lovely, furious...and awkward. Your first time's not going to be a bodice-ripping, explosive—"

"Grandma!" I cried.

"—amazing thing right away," she said. "Just be patient, with yourself and with Jon."

I stopped outside the dining hall, closed my eyes, and nodded, thinking maybe I really was sadistic for having this conversation with her, but maybe Grandma was also a genius.

"Number two. Please be safe. There are more options for you now than I had when I was your age, and I would hate to see you and Jon put yourselves in a life-changing situation if it wasn't absolutely necessary."

"Right," I agreed.

"And three." She paused. "Don't do anything you're not ready for. If Jon's a good boy, like I think he is, he'll understand."

I hoped, with all my heart, she was right.

Eric waved a hand in front of my face.

I pointed at my phone and mouthed, "I'll meet you inside."

He shrugged. "I can wait."

Well, I guess that was that for my conversation with Grandma. "Thanks for talking. I'll call you later?"

"Sure, honey. I love you."

"Love you too."

I hung up and put the phone in my pocket, giving Eric what I hoped looked like a sincere smile. "Sorry."

"That's fine." He held the door open for me. "Talking to your parents?"

"Yeah," I lied, stepping in behind him.

"How are they doing?"

"Great." Could we change the subject?

"Good," he said.

"I'm going to grab some food, and I'll meet you at

the table?"

I took my time finding vegetables and healthy protein for my salad before going to sit with Eric. I was so ready for this project to be over. It wasn't anything against him; I would just much rather be spending my lunch with Jon.

He looked up at me from behind his laptop lid and smiled. "I think we're almost done. Just need to review."

"Let me see it," I said, sitting down. I glanced over the slides and compared what we had on the screen to my notes from class. We'd done alright. Solid B work, at least.

I marked notes in the comment sections for which parts I would talk about and which were his responsibility and then spun it back to him.

"Anything else?" I asked.

"I don't think so." He sighed, shutting his laptop. "We're good for tomorrow anyway." His eyes went to my plate that was still full of vegetables hurriedly plucked from the salad bar. "What are you, a rabbit?"

I shoved my plate away. "No, just trying to eat healthy."

He nodded at his plate that held the remnants of cheese and greasy meat-covered corn chips. "You're making me look bad."

"Don't you mean the saturated fat is?"

His hand covered his chest. "You wound me."

I rolled my eyes. "So sensitive."

"Don't girls like the sensitive guys?"

"I wouldn't know." Jon wasn't what I would call sensitive. More like kind, caring, compassionate, strong...

"You're daydreaming again."

This time, my cheeks heated.

"So, why did you skip the bar early last night?" he asked. "I was hoping for another dance, you know. The risk to my feet would be worth it."

"Just needed some air," I hedged. The lie came easily. It seemed like I was lying more than ever, always to protect someone else. Couldn't they see I was the one who needed protecting? But I would have to let someone in first for that to happen.

I put my notebook in my backpack. "Are we good?"

He nodded. "See you in class?"

"See you in class."

I went right back to my room after lunch. As I walked up the stairs to my dorm—a way I found to sneak in some extra exercise—I began feeling light-headed. God, I needed to get more sleep. These late nights were too much for me, especially with Coach Cadence killing us in practice.

I had to stop on the sixth floor, but eventually I made it up to my room and collapsed into my deckchair. I rested my forehead on the cool surface of the desk, and some paper pressed into the edge of my skin. As I pulled back, the envelope stuck to my forehead, then fell before me.

Another note with my name front and center. I ripped it open and read the words.

Starving yourself won't make him stay.

My eyes narrowed at the page. The message was too familiar.

This had gone too far. There was no way this was a prankster who didn't know when to quit. No, this was personal, and I knew just who it was.

I sent Grandma a quick text and told her I wouldn't be home until Saturday afternoon instead of Saturday morning.

I had someone to see.

CHAPTER THIRTY-NINE

I HOOKED my thumbs in my pockets as Jon put his bags into the passenger seat of his car. He planned to meet his parents in Woodman this afternoon and ride with them to Dallas.

A whole weekend without Jon.

But maybe it was better this way.

He wouldn't be privy to my drama. The perpetual crap show that was my life. The more I thought about it, the less I wanted him to come with me to the prison. What if he saw where I came from and recognized some of that chaos in me?

Jon traced his thumb over my chin, and I turned my eyes up at him.

"What's going on in there?" He kissed my forehead.

I breathed in his touch. "Too much."

His lips formed a smile against my skin. "As usual."

I lifted a corner of my lips and pulled back.

His hands cupped my face as he looked at me, taking me in.

"I'm going to miss you," I said.

"I always miss you."

"Even now?"

His lips turned into a smile. "Every second you're not in my arms is a second wasted."

"Then fix it," I breathed.

He held me close, and I hung on to him, trying to gather all his love and support before I made a trip to see the most wicked person in my life and put a stop to these notes.

When his lips found mine, I kissed him back, hungry for all he could give me. He was everything. My everything when I had nothing. We got lost in each other, in the moment, in the feel of our lips exploring and tasting.

Breathing hard with heavy-lidded eyes, Jon said, "I'll see you on Sunday night."

The space between us grew as he stepped back and got into his car. I stood in the parking lot until he'd gotten onto the main road and then started walking back to the dorms.

If running had taught me anything, it was that I needed to keep going to keep the pain from catching up with me. Because if I stopped, it would be right there, ready to drag me down.

CHAPTER FORTY

ANIKA AND KYLE had already left by the time I made it back to our room. There was a note from Anika on my desk that said *Have a great weekend!*

Guilt swept through me. I was kind of a crappy roommate. Anika and I should have been building a friendship, but instead I was obsessing over my never-ending list of problems.

Mo' money mo' problems?

More like mo' messed up parents in jail on drug charges mo' festering anxiety that touched every part of your life. Or something like that.

Evan was right. Everyone built up college like it was some castle you went off to after high school graduation, where you would automatically meet friends and have fun and "find yourself." Whatever that meant.

I knew who I was. That was the problem. I was the daughter of two convicts. A recently obese teenager. An average student. And now a below-average member of the track team.

The girlfriend of a guy who was probably seconds away from realizing how good he was and leaving me.

I needed to stop thinking like that. He chose me. That was his choice. I hadn't forced him into that. He could have had any girl. Had Denise. And passed.

If I weren't pulling my weight (however much of it there was) on the track team, there were other qualified girls lined up for the spot.

So here I was, this broken vase with the gold filling, alone in my dorm room for the evening. For the first time in a long time, I wasn't afraid because I knew the sender was trapped behind bars. She could send notes all she wanted, but there was no way she was coming anywhere near this campus.

Part of me wanted the night to last forever because I knew what tomorrow would bring. Another part—probably my stomach—ached with nerves, wishing I could just get this over with.

I called Nikki and asked if she'd meet me in the dining hall for supper. I needed a distraction.

When I arrived, she was already waiting by the check-in counter, texting.

"Hey," I said, giving her a smile.

She eyed me. "Are you tired?"

My cheeks warmed. "Gee, thanks."

"No, really," she said. "You look anemic. We're getting you a steak."

I shoved my hands in my sweatpants pockets, uncomfortable. "You mean mystery meat?" I tried to joke.

She handed her card to the person swiping everyone into the dining hall. "Come on."

I followed her in, and she made sure I got a big helping of stir-fry meat from the wok and lots of leafy green vegetables. At least she didn't push it on the salad dressing.

We sat down, and she put her elbows on the surface of the table, using her teeth to open a packet of ketchup. "Why don't they have a dispenser like everywhere else?"

I picked at a piece of the meat with my fork and shrugged. When it entered my mouth, it felt slimy— chewy. I barely managed to swallow it.

"Big plans for the weekend?" Nikki asked.

Oh, you know, just seeing my mom, who wants me dead, to confront her about a few threatening letters. "Define big," I said instead.

She laughed. "What, are you losing your v-card or something?"

I stared at my plate, trying not to let the heat in my cheeks show. "Don't call it that."

"So you are?" She gushed. "You and your guy looked pretty close at the bar!"

I lifted my gaze and shook my head. "No, that wasn't my boyfriend."

She raised her eyebrows.

"Just some guy from class," I said.

"Sure."

"What about you?" I asked.

"Work, work, and..." Her eyes darted back and forth across the room, making sure no one was listening to us. "Oh yeah, more work."

I laughed. "Seriously?"

"Yeah, it's my dad's rule," she said. "He pays for my pickup and gas and a little spending money here and there, and I help him out on breaks."

A pang of jealousy swept through me. I wished I had a dad who supported me at all. I reached for my phone, for a distraction from this, and saw the date.

A year ago today, my dad beat me so bad even the thickest foundation couldn't hide the proof.

A year ago tomorrow, I started school at Woodman. Met Jon. Sat at the lunch table with Stormy.

"What?" Nikki asked.

I shook my head, blinking my eyes fast at the moisture that had suddenly appeared there.

"You can tell me," she said, her eyes wide, earnest.

"I…" I covered my mouth. "It's a long story."

She gestured at my plate. "You have lots left to eat. We clearly have time."

CHAPTER FORTY-ONE

I WENT BACK to my room, feeling freer and lighter somehow now that Nikki knew my secret. If you could call it that. I could see it in her eyes that she didn't understand what I'd been through—but she cared, and that was more than enough.

After I'd changed and gotten into bed with my laptop, ready to veg out with some television, my phone vibrated with a text message.

Stormy: I can't wait to see you tomorrow!

Stormy: Miss you chica :)

I smiled at the screen and sent a reply. Somehow, I felt so far away from Stormy and my life in Woodman, even though I was only an hour away.

I thought of my friends and what they were doing right now. Roberto would be back in

Woodman for the first time since basic training. Evan and Michele were probably on a date, catching up. Frank and Stormy had to be spending time together. And Andrew and Skye? They wouldn't be home until the semester break since flights were so expensive.

Spending time with the group wouldn't feel the same without them. Without Jon.

He and his parents were probably close to Dallas by now. I took a deep breath and called his number.

After a few rings, he answered. And so did his parents.

"Hi, Abi," Glen said.

"Hi, sweetheart," Marta chimed in.

"You're on the car phone," Jon explained.

"Oh, hi." I tried to make my voice just the right amount of sympathetic. "Mr. Scoller, how's your cousin doing?"

"She's stable at least," he said. "Bad case of pancreatitis. The doctor said these things can turn at any minute, so..." His voice cracked. "We needed to pay her a visit."

"Of course," I replied. "I hope she gets better."

"Me too," he said.

The rush of wind against their car was the only sound for a moment until Marta said, "Abi, tell us about college, your classes? Jon said you've been working hard on a group project?"

"Yeah, we presented earlier today, and I think it went okay!" Prof Warren had actually told us good job afterwards, not sarcastically either, which was kind of rare for her. "They started me out with twelve credit hours since I'm in track and had kind of a rough last year of high school. I have a few friends on the track team, and my roommate is actually from Roderdale."

"Good job, sweetie!" Marta commended. "Jon told me your roommate is his roommate's girlfriend?"

"Yes! Isn't that weird?"

"A strange co-inky-dink for sure." She laughed. "Just don't go switching rooms for hanky panky."

"Mom," Jon groaned at the same time I buried my face in my pillow and tried not to die right there of embarrassment.

"Just teasing," she said. "Well, it sounds like things are going great for you. It's about time."

My lips twitched. They *were* going well. Except for the busyness of it all. And the threatening letters. And the fact that Jon knew nothing about it. I needed to tell him. Before I left in the morning.

"Jon, I—" I began at the same time Mr. Scoller

said, "Sorry, sweetie, we're pulling into the hospital! We love you!"

The line went silent and I stared at my phone, waiting. If Jon texted me, I would tell him, just get it over with. But he didn't. He had bigger things to worry about, like his cousin that was practically on her deathbed and his dad who was losing someone close enough to be a sibling.

Eventually, I turned my phone off and fell into a restless sleep. Tomorrow would bring its own challenges, and I needed my strength to deal with them.

CHAPTER FORTY-TWO

WHEN I COULDN'T STAY in bed any longer—
around six in the morning—I dressed in the most
bland, prison-visit-approved clothing I could find,
made some coffee in the knock-off one-cup
coffeemaker Anika brought, and then stepped into
the hallway, lugging all my things for the weekend.

Nikki sat on the floor, right outside my door.

I staggered back, gripping my heart. "What the
hell are you doing here?"

Standing up, she giggled. "Scared you?"

Rolling my eyes, I set my duffle down and folded
my arms across my chest. "Not at all. I almost have a
heart attack every time I leave my dorm room."

She patted my arm. "You'll be okay."

Silence hung between us for a moment as I stared at her, waiting for an explanation.

"Oh!" she said, like she frequently terrified the crap out of people in the morning. "You want to know why I'm here." She gestured at my bag. "I know this is hard for you, and I just wanted to be there with you."

I opened my mouth to argue, but she kept going.

"You shouldn't have to do this by yourself, even if you want to."

I thought of whether it would be possible to argue with her, but judging by the set of her chin, the odds were against me.

"You can ride along," I finally said, "but they won't let you in to see my mom."

"That's fine," she said. "Now, grab those letters."

"What?" My blood chilled just thinking of them.

"If it's her sending them, you need to turn them in to the warden. I did some research, and this type of thing could affect whether or not she gets parole."

"Seriously?" My eyes widened at the thought of my mom being released from prison. In my mind, I was here, and she was there. We wouldn't meet again.

But these notes—and the very real possibility of parole—suggested something different.

Nikki nodded. "Might even get her a longer sentence, honestly, if those notes are as bad as you said they were."

Wow. With shaky hands, I unlocked the dorm room door and went inside to my desk. I pulled open the bottom drawer, lifted out a heavy biology textbook I'd yet to use, and gathered the pile of letters.

They had all the weight of a poisonous snake ready to strike, and I shoved them into an empty folder so I wouldn't have to see them anymore. I tried not to watch Nikki's eyes, I really did, but I couldn't miss the overwhelmed, terrified, pitying look that was there.

She quickly replaced it with a placid smile. "We'll get this figured out, girl. I promise."

It was an empty promise, but it made me feel better, less alone, to know someone cared other than Grandma and some random salesperson.

We walked together to the parking lot in mostly silence. It was early enough that hardly anyone was awake. I liked the campus best this way. It reminded me of my morning runs in Woodman. Of coming back into the house to Grandma reading her newspaper and offering me hot green tea.

My yellow bug came into view, a shiny spot in the sea of vehicles. "This is mine," I said.

She giggled. "Sticks out like a sore thumb. Like mine."

"Hey," I said, "don't compare my baby to your rust bucket."

"Rust bucket?" She feigned offense. "How dare you call Priscilla a rust bucket!"

"You named that thing Priscilla?"

With an embarrassed, tight-lipped smile, she nodded.

I laughed. "Irony. I like it."

I put my key in the trunk at the front of the car and loaded up my things before unlocking the doors and getting inside.

"This is cute," Nikki said.

"I love it." I ran my fingers over the keychain Mr. Pelosi had gotten me before putting my key in the ignition. Even if I couldn't have him as a teacher, I still had his wisdom—the things he'd taught me.

I typed the address to the prison into my GPS, and we started the two-hour drive to see my mother.

"It's in the middle of nowhere," I told Nikki.

"Yeah, I looked it up last night," she admitted. "So she's been in there for a year?"

"Not quite," I said. "I think they kept her in the county jail for a while before she was sentenced."

Her lips formed an "oh." And that was it before her next question broke the silence. "What are you going to say to her when you see her?"

"Isn't that the million-dollar question."

CHAPTER FORTY-THREE

THE CLOSER WE got to the prison, the more my heart sped and my hands shook. I could see the brick building looming out of the ground from a mile away. It stood solitary, away from the town so the women inside would be as separated from society as possible.

Didn't they know even if they stuck them on the moon it wouldn't be far enough away?

I parked in the nearly empty parking lot, leaving my hands on the wheel and staring straight ahead.

"Are you okay?" Nikki asked.

A quick shake of my head indicated my answer.

"Just nervous?"

Just? I was seconds from collapsing into a pile and never getting up again. This whole thing had been a hare-brained idea. She was in jail. It wasn't like she could do anything to me from inside the walls of this building, trapped within the chain-link fence and spiraling barbed wire. Was it really worth seeing her again just to confront her about the letters?

"What would happen if we went back to the college?" I asked.

Nikki paused for a moment before shifting in her seat and putting a hand on my shoulder. "You don't have to be here, you know. You could turn those letters in to the cops now that you think it's her and let them investigate it. But you haven't yet. Admit it; some part of you wants to confront her on your own and put a stop to this."

I breathed deeply. She was right. I'd needed to go in there and confront my mom. But that didn't make letting go of the steering wheel and getting out of the car any easier.

"I've seen you run ten miles without stopping and lift weights like a freakin' boss," Nikki said. "You can take on some coward who beat up on a teenage girl with wire hangers and sent these notes."

There was a fire in her voice that caught on my soul. It was just enough to make me open the car door, get inside, and drive to the prison.

There weren't many people in the waiting room.

I bet they would start filtering in soon, though, with it being a holiday weekend. I stepped forward to the receptionist, and this time, I was ready for the skeptical look she gave me behind the glass.

I didn't belong here, but she didn't know that.

After thirty minutes of waiting in silence beside Nikki, a CO came back and got me. He searched me in a holding room. Wove a wand over my body. Checked that my bra didn't have any wires. Looked over my clothes for signs of logos or too much skin.

My body might have been there for the examination, but my mind was somewhere else. Another room over to be exact. To the woman with the sunken eyes and lank hair and a tongue that could do just as much damage as any weapon.

"I don't have all day," the CO grunted, waiting by the door.

My eyes snapped to where he stood. "Sorry," I mumbled and followed him.

We walked back to the same visiting room as when I went with Grandma, but it looked so different this time. Now, I knew the prison was her home. Where my mother belonged. A reflection of her life and her choices. Not of me. At least, I hoped.

He sat me down at the table farthest from the two other families visiting. There were children with their dad and someone who was clearly a caseworker with a clipboard and business casual dress clothes. Then a couple, holding hands across the table. The guy had tattoos wrapped around his arm and all the way up his neck.

And then the door opened, and my mother walked in.

She wasn't beautiful anymore. Not even close. She appeared dead, drained, in every sense of the word. Even her skin looked squalid.

The CO kept his hand on her back until she sat down across from me. She shrugged away from him, and he grunted as he walked away.

Those death-incarnate, drilling eyes turned on me, and her voice came out as threatening as a snake's hiss. "To what do I owe this visit, darling daughter?"

"Cut the crap," I said.

Her eyes showed a spark of life as she leaned back and folded her arms across her chest. "What, no show of the perfect Abigail when your grandma's not around to watch you?"

I ignored her comment. "I came to tell you to stop sending the notes."

"What notes?"

"Don't play dumb," I snapped. "You know

exactly what notes. I don't know how you got my new address, but I'm tired of seeing them. If you've got something to say to me, say it right now."

"Oh, I've got plenty to say to you," she said, disinterested. "But it might take all day. What's in it for me?"

I rolled my eyes.

Her voice turned sickly sweet. "Don't you roll your eyes at your mother, *precious girl.*"

"Stop it," I whisper-yelled. "Listen, I'm telling you to stop, and if you don't, I will report the letters to the police and you'll be in here even longer."

I fought to hide the shake in my voice. Being here, around my mom, around the life I worked so hard to escape—it ate at me.

"I don't know what you're talking about," she deadpanned

"Really? 'You won't last six months.' 'Starving yourself won't make him stay.' You've been sending me these ridiculous letters since graduation."

Her mouth tightened in a hard line. "I don't like being accused of things I didn't do."

"Well that's good, because you did do this," I retorted, struggling to keep my voice down. "And I'm tired of it. Get the hell out of my life!"

She stood up.

As the CO walked over to get her, she spat, "Then get the hell out of mine."

I sucked in deep breaths as they escorted me back to the waiting area. Last time I'd been here, I'd passed out, been overwhelmed, had blood dripping down my cheek from my mother's assault.

Now, my only wounds were mental. The reminder of where I came from. The fear of the future. And now the confusion of not knowing who had sent the letters. Because I knew how my mother looked when she lied. She had been telling the truth.

The second I walked into the lobby and Nikki saw me, she stood up. "Did she—"

I shook my head, indicating we should wait until we got outside to discuss it. Who knew who was listening here.

I waited to speak until we were in my car and on the road. "I don't know who's been sending those letters, but it wasn't my mom."

CHAPTER FORTY-FOUR

NIKKI and I spent the rest of the trip trying to think of who it could be, but I had no idea. My dad hadn't spoken to me since he'd been in prison. There was no way for him to know where I lived, especially now that I was in college. Plus, I'd flown so far under the radar in McClellan and Woodman, there was no reason for anyone to hate me.

"Could it be someone at the college?" she asked.

I snorted. "You mean out of the five people that know I exist?"

She gave me the side-eye.

"You know, now that I think about it, Prof Warren was pretty mad about me being late to class the first day."

She popped my shoulder. "Seriously," she said. "You should bring them to the police."

"What for?" I asked. "They already told my grandma there's nothing they can do if I don't know who it is."

She lifted her hands in exasperation. "I don't know. Maybe you can ask them to keep patrol cars around the college, just in case? This is scary, Abi."

I fought the fear rising in my own chest, making acid swirl in my stomach. "It's probably just a prank," I tried to convince myself. "I'll be fine."

From the twist of her lips and the way she was ringing her hands, she didn't believe me. "Fine. But you should get a gun."

I snorted at the ridiculousness of the idea, then jingled my keychain, which now had the defense attachment and pepper spray right next to my Einstein quote. "I'm good."

She seemed skeptical but kept her thoughts to herself. That was fine, because I had plenty of my own.

If the letters weren't coming from my mom, they were coming from someone who knew my address before and after I started college. That was a pretty limited number of people, none of whom I could even dream would write those letters to me. Or give my address to someone who would.

Unless someone had been watching me. Just the thought sent chills through my skin, making me feel dirty, exposed. Having Nikki here right now was the only thing keeping complete panic at bay. "Thanks for coming," I said.

"Any time. Really." Her lips twitched. "Do you mind if I ask you something?"

My hands tensed on the steering wheel, but I made my face a mask. "Sure. What?"

"Why haven't you told your boyfriend what's going on?"

"The truth?" I asked, keeping my eyes straight ahead.

"Yeah," she said softly.

"Because." I took a breath. Another one. "My boyfriend has enough to worry about without adding me to the mix."

She let it drop, and we rode quietly the rest of the way home, the radio filling the space around us.

When we got back to the college, Nikki showed me where she'd parked "Priscilla."

I pulled alongside her vehicle and looked over at her. I realized she was my first real, true friend at college, and my heart swelled more than I was comfortable with. I didn't want to scare her away. "See you at practice Monday?"

"For sure," she said. "And let your grandma feed you when you're home. I know you've been stressed, but you have to keep your energy up."

I told her I would, even though my stomach had other feelings about food at the moment.

The second she left the car, I felt so much more alone, vulnerable. I hurriedly put my car in gear and started the drive home, checking my rearview mirror along the way to make sure no one was following me.

My phone rang, and Jon's name appeared across the screen. My shoulders immediately relaxed as I held the phone to my ear and said, "Hello?"

"Hi, beautiful," he breathed.

This. This was what I needed to hear.

"How are you?" I asked. "How's your cousin?"

He paused, and I heard him blow out a heavy breath. "It's not looking good, Abs. She's in so much pain."

I hated to hear that she was in pain, hated the hurting clear in his own voice. "What can I do?"

"Just...talk to me? I miss you."

A smile quirked my lips. "I miss you too."

"Tell me what you did this morning. What you're going to do when you get home."

"Oh..." I stuttered. "I, um, hung out with Nikki this morning. Drove around." It was close to the truth.

"That sounds fun," he said. "See, I told you you'd make friends."

"You were right," I said. "Is that what you wanted to hear?"

"Always." He laughed. "What about tonight? I can't believe I'm missing Roberto being home." Regret twisted through his words. "I feel like I needed to be here, though."

"There will be other times," I reassured, trying to comfort him. "I'm not sure what we're doing, but I think Stormy has a plan."

He chuckled. "As usual."

I loved that my friends had become *our* friends. It made me feel even more connected to him. "And I'm going to get some time in with Grandma on Sunday. I think we're going antiquing."

"Her whole house is an antique."

I laughed. That was true. "She just doesn't throw things away until she's gotten the goodie out of it. Technically, she's an environmentalist."

That made him laugh. "Sure."

"Come on. You can't be judging. Your mom gave

you a needlepoint to hang up in your room that says 'dorm sweet dorm.'"

"Shh," he hurriedly said. "You're ruining my street cred."

"With who, you goodie-two-shoes?"

"Hey, I prefer socially responsible."

"Yeah, yeah," I said.

Voices sounded in the background on Jon's phone.

"Sorry," he said, "I gotta go. I love you."

The call had already ended by the time I said it back.

CHAPTER FORTY-FIVE

SOON, the huge grain elevators on the outside of Woodman appeared on the horizon, and a weight that had been on my shoulders since the day I left lifted.

Home.

This was home.

First on my agenda? Going to Stormy's to see my friends. We had to hang out during the day because Stormy had taken the closing shift at the restaurant, and things just weren't the same without her.

Honestly, I wouldn't even have these friends without her.

When I started down her street, I saw most of the guys standing around Frank's Suburban with the tailgate up. A massive red cooler sat inside. Stormy walked down the sidewalk with Leanne and Macy, carrying roasting pans wrapped in foil.

We hadn't talked about specifics, but it seemed like they had a pretty big plan going. What were they up to?

Roberto saw me first and pointed, a grin splitting his face. The others followed his stare and waved at me. It felt like that day in the cafeteria all over again when I walked up to see them applauding me. Telling me I was *in*.

I honked at them, then parked on the opposite end of the street, facing the wrong way. Being back in Woodman was great. I could never do that in Austin.

Stormy set her pan down and ran to hug me first, wrapping me in her slender arms.

"*Chica!*" Stormy said, pulling back to look at me. "Damn, you're looking *fine*."

I rolled my eyes. "You're going to make Frank jealous."

"He should be jealous!" She waved her arms at the others. "Look how ripped Abi is!"

"Okay, okay." I wrapped my arms around my middle. She just couldn't see all the loose skin and fat hiding underneath the modest clothes I had to wear to the prison. "Can we talk about someone else? Roberto! Look at your hair!"

He had little patterns shaved into the side of his head.

"It looks so cool," I said.

Macy rubbed her hands over the side. "Feels cool, too!"

Soon we were all rubbing Roberto's head and he was running away, and we were chasing him in the street like kids with a loose ball, not a care in the world.

A car honked at us, the man inside shaking his head like this was the exact reason he had a "STAY OFF MY YARD" sign in front of his house.

We laughed, and the others started getting into Frank's Suburban.

"Where are we going?" I asked.

"Fishing hole," Stormy said. "You got a suit?"

I shook my head. "I didn't know we'd be going anywhere."

"I brought an extra," Leanne said. "Just in case."

I shrugged and got in the car, taking a seat in the middle row by Evan and Michele. At least he sat in the middle. I couldn't be imagining the death stares Michele kept sending my way when Evan wasn't looking.

I decided to change my focus and twisted in my seat so I could see Roberto, Macy, and Leanne in the back seat. "Tell us about basic, Roberto."

He gave me a lopsided smile. "What do you want to know?"

Frank shouted from the front. "Tell her about the toothbrushes!"

"Shit." Roberto looked out the side of the car. "Those sergeants are hard-asses, *guera*, like you have no idea. Worse than Mrs. Delby. Some of the guys were a little slow to get out of bed, and you know what they made us do?

I shifted so I could see him better. "What?"

"They had us go get our toothbrushes and scrub the entire floor."

"Ew." I made a face, and the others who hadn't already heard the story let out similar expressions.

Michele asked, "What did you do with your toothbrushes?"

"You get one toothbrush," he said. "After a few days, you get pretty desperate and clean it out."

"Any hot girls there?" Frank yelled from the front.

Roberto acted like he was about to throw up. "But ten weeks was too long for some people."

My brows came together. "What do you mean?"

He shook his head. "I was walking by this dumpster, and I heard something in there. Thought it was a rat or something."

Macy's eyes widened. "No."

"Yep." He nodded. "Puts a whole new meaning to the phrase 'getting nasty.'"

"Ew," I said. "Stop."

"What?" He smirked. "You have a problem with me talking about someone getting down and dirty?"

"Stooop!" I cried. "New subject. Anyone?"

"Speaking of getting nasty," Stormy said.

"Not you too," I said.

She laughed. "What about you and Jon?"

I wiped my face of all expression. "What about me and Jon?"

Roberto leaned over. "You pound?"

I turned to him, incredulous. "Pound?"

"You don't know what that means?"

Flustered, I said, "Yes, I know what it means. Why would you call it that?"

He quirked an eyebrow. "Is that a yes?"

"Let's talk about Evan and Michele," I said. "What about them? Have they 'pounded'?"

Roberto burst out laughing, Michele covered her face with her hair, and Evan gave me a dirty stare.

"Gee, thanks, Abi," he droned.

I lifted my hands. "A girl's gotta do what a girl's gotta do."

"You mean who," Roberto corrected.

"I hate you."

Evan leaned forward to the front seat. "Are we there yet?"

Frank turned into a pasture. "Just in time. Grab the gate."

Evan popped his door open and said a relieved, "Thank you," shutting the door behind him.

Michele yelled after him, "Don't leave me here!"

Roberto steepled his fingers like an evil mastermind. "So, Michele. You take our boy's v-card? We all know Abi didn't."

Macy shoved him. "It's already awkward enough, dude."

Roberto sat back, laughing, but I didn't miss the glare Michele sent my way.

CHAPTER FORTY-SIX

FRANK PARKED alongside a big pond in the middle of a pasture. As we got out of the car and stepped into the tall prairie grass, grasshoppers flew through the air, trying to get away from us.

A light wind swished the plains, adding a sweet rustling sound to that of my friends getting ready for the day. Frank and Evan went to the trunk, taking out the cooler. Stormy organized food in the tailgate like a table, and Macy started huffing into a pool float.

The others began shimmying out of their clothes, undressing down to their swimsuits.

The last time we'd undressed, we were under totally different circumstances.

"I think I've only seen you guys half-naked at the cemetery," I said, laughing.

Stormy waggled her eyebrows at me. "We should change that, *chica*."

I rolled my eyes and went to the tailgate to help Macy with one of the floats. As I emptied my lungs, a giant rainbow unicorn came to life. Just as I finished hooking the plug shut, Roberto grabbed it and crashed into the pond, spraying water everywhere. Frank did the same with Macy's float, and we laughed at the two. They were so ridiculous, romping in the water like little kids going to the pool for the first time all summer.

Evan and Michele held hands and started toward the water.

Stormy came to stand beside me. "Tell me you don't like her," she whispered.

I shrugged and turned back to the tailgate, reaching for another float. "I don't really know her. Other than the fact that she apparently hates me."

She leaned back against the bumper, arms folded over her chest. "She's just jealous."

With my teeth bitten down on the hole, I asked, "Why would she be?"

"Oh, come on," Stormy said. "Here's Evan's ex-girlfriend, who's a super-hot track star with legs for days, and she's just a short little junior in high school. It's a little intimidating."

I rolled my eyes and blew a huge breath into the float. "I'm dating Jon."

"That doesn't mean Freckles doesn't like you."

My mouth fell off the float. "He doesn't like me."

"No, but Michele doesn't know that."

I shook my head and sighed. "How does a junior in high school seem so young to me now?"

She tilted her head, examining the two tiptoeing into the water. "She does seem young, doesn't she?"

I nodded.

We worked together blowing up the last of the floats, and then I changed into the swimsuit Leanne left in the Suburban. It was a little more revealing than I would have liked, but it was that or underwear.

Stormy caught me tugging at the swimsuit and said, "You look great. Come on."

She stuck her hand out, and I took it, walking into the water with her. It was warm on top from the sun beating down, but the deeper we got, the cooler and more refreshing it felt.

We all lay around on floats, or in Frank and Evan's case, hung on to them like Jack on the Titanic door. At least Stormy and Michele wouldn't let them sink to their death.

We drifted between topics as we drifted on the water, never talking about anything serious or hard. Just catching up on where we'd been and what we'd been doing.

Macy and Leanne had joined the improv team at their college. Evan started working at a chain restaurant and had already been promoted to shift leader. Roberto would go to his new assignment in North Carolina in a week. Frank had almost quit his job and got a two-dollar raise instead.

But Stormy threw a curveball. "Guys," she said, holding on tightly to Frank's hand. "I have to tell you something."

I sat up as well as one could on an inflatable popsicle. Something told me this was serious.

Macy furrowed her eyebrows. "Everything okay?"

"Yeah, it's just..." She looked at Frank, and he gave her an encouraging nod. "I'm pregnant."

CHAPTER FORTY-SEVEN

MY MOUTH FELL OPEN, frozen, while my mind went on hyperdrive. Pregnant? "With a baby?" I finally asked.

She rolled her eyes like this wasn't the biggest news of the entire year. "No, with emotion."

Macy reached over and swatted her. "Seriously? Pregnant?"

My eyes zoned in on her stomach. Was I just imagining a bump?

"Yes," she said.

"Are you sure?" Evan asked.

Frank nodded. "She peed on, like, four tests."

"I had to be positive," Stormy said, a little bashfully. "We have our first sonogram on Tuesday."

"Wow," I breathed. "A baby."

Suddenly, it struck me how different our lives were. Like Stormy and Frank had somehow jumped lightyears ahead of all of us. They were about to become parents, working full-time jobs, paying utility bills, health insurance, food. The sheer idea of all they'd have to take on overwhelmed me.

"Are you okay?" I asked.

Her arms loosely circled her stomach like she was cradling the baby growing there. "I love her... him...it already."

Frank smiled softly as he put a hand on her stomach. "And I'm here for them always." He dropped a soft kiss on her forehead, and Stormy closed her eyes.

The moment felt so private, so intimate, I looked down at the water. It rippled slowly, oblivious to the earth-rocking news we'd just heard.

"Well, in that case," Roberto said. "Congratulations!" He went over and shook Frank's shoulder, then wrapped him in a wet bro hug.

We all paddled over and hugged them, telling them congratulations and that we were there to help them however we could.

That was just our group. No matter where we went, how different our lives were, we were there for each other. I wished Jon had been here for this moment. I imagined him wrapping his arm around me and smiling. Then I shoved down thoughts of us celebrating the same thing years in the future.

Which made me feel that much worse for keeping my secret from everyone. They were being brave, sharing something that so many people kept secret and were ashamed of.

I needed to tell the truth about my secrets. But I would wait until later. This moment was Frank and Stormy's. They deserved to enjoy it.

CHAPTER FORTY-EIGHT

I GOT BACK to Grandma's around seven. The freshly mowed front yard and waving Upton U flag nearly brought me to tears. I couldn't wait to get inside. I missed her so much.

It took all I had not to run down the sidewalk, but Grandma beat me to it, opening the front door and coming to wrap me in a tight hug.

"Oh, sweetie, it's good to see you," she said, not letting go.

I held her close, choking back tears. "I missed you so much."

All of the stress from that day—seeing my mom, the letters, missing Jon, Frank and Stormy's announcement—it all came crashing down and pouring through my eyes.

"Honey, honey, honey." She rubbed my back. "It's okay. I'm here."

She comforted me like I was five years old, and I let her, rocking back and forth on the sidewalk, leaning into this woman who had been my rock though she didn't have to be.

When my tears finally subsided, she took one of my hands with both of hers, patting it, and said, "Come on, let's get inside."

I'd grown so used to living at Grandma's, I'd forgotten it had a smell. But it did. Like green tea and vanilla and old wood. I breathed it in deep. This was the smell of home.

We walked into the living room, and I stalled in the doorway.

"What is this?" I asked, staring at the brand-new sectional.

Grandma's old rocking recliner was gone, as was the threadbare mustard sofa that had been there before. A new leather sectional with cupholders emitting blue light took up the space instead.

"What do you think?" she asked, going to sit on it. She pushed a button, making the leg rest rise and waggled her eyebrows at me. Her face lit up like she'd just finished the hardest crossword puzzle ever.

Laughing, I went and sat on the other reclining

seat. "Fancy, Grandma." The seat sank underneath me, comfortable, but not like twenty years of butts had softened it up for me.

"Had to spruce up a little before my girl came home," she said. "Plus, I thought we could watch a movie together to break it in? Your pick."

The hope in her voice melted my heart. "Of course."

While she made snacks, I checked my phone. Jon had texted me a few hours ago, but I missed it in all the day's activities.

Jon: How is it being home?

Abi: Amazing.

Abi: Grandma and I are going to watch a movie, so I probably can't talk on the phone.

Abi: Oh, and Stormy's pregnant.

Abi: They're happy about it.

Abi: They look really good.

Abi: Roberto had this gross story about basic training and dumpsters.

Abi: Macy and Leanne are on an improv team.

Abi: Evan's crushing it at work.

Abi: His girlfriend hates me.

Jon: Whoa girl, you're blowing up my phone.

Abi: Did you just call me girl?

Jon: Do you prefer woman?

Abi: Eyeroll emoji.

Jon: I miss you. Send me a picture?

Abi: I don't have any makeup on. Plus my hair's a total wreck.

Jon: I don't care. Just want to see your smile.

Jon: It's rough here.

My heart went out to him. I snapped a picture of the biggest, cheesiest smile I could muster and sent it to him.

Jon: Perfection.

Abi: I love you.

Jon: I love you. So much.

The microwave went off in the other room and Grandma came back in. "Texting Jon?"

"Yeah," I said.

"How's Glen's cousin?" she asked. "Marta said it wasn't looking good when I talked to her yesterday."

"That's what Jon said this morning. Let me check again."

She nodded and went about choosing a DVD to put in the player while I texted Jon.

Abi: How are things there? How's your cousin?

Jon: The doctors can't get her levels to come down. They say her kidneys are shutting down.

"Oh no," I breathed, covering my heart with my hand. "He said her kidneys are shutting down."

Worry covered Grandma's face. "Tell him I'm praying for her. And his family."

It seemed like a small comfort to someone who was watching a family member in pain, but it was the best we could do from here.

Abi: Grandma wants you to know she's praying for your family and your cousin.

Jon: Tell her thank you. I just hope the pain doesn't last long, whatever happens.

I cringed at the message, eyeing Grandma over my phone as she bent over the DVD rack. I was all she had left, other than the Scollers. I couldn't imagine watching her suffer.

Abi: Me too.

Jon: Enjoy your night with your grandma. And call me in the morning. I love you.

I tucked my phone in my pocket and settled back in the chair as the opening credits started on the screen. Grandma grabbed a couple of well-worn blankets and threw one over me. I curled into it and leaned on the couch's center console.

Grandma sat on the other side, holding my hand. "I'm so glad you're home."

"Me too."

We fell asleep watching the movie, and I woke

up to my phone ringing at four in the morning. A call from Jon.

My heart immediately leapt to hyper speed as I swiped answer and held the phone to my ear. "Jon?"

"She died, Abi," he said, and then he broke down in sobs.

CHAPTER FORTY-NINE

"JON, I'm so sorry. I'm so sorry." I whispered the words over and over until his sobs died down, feeling completely helpless.

I should have gone with him, should have insisted on it. But now he was suffering by himself on the other end of the phone, and there was nothing I could do about it.

Grandma shifted beside me, coming to with a concerned look in her eyes.

She died, I mouthed.

Grandma covered her mouth.

"It's okay," Jon rasped, sniffing.

"It's not," I said. "I can't imagine how you must feel."

"My dad's even worse," he said. "Wouldn't leave the room. He watched it happen."

"Oh God," I breathed.

"I just...needed to hear your voice," he said.

My heart swelled and shattered. "I'm here. Always."

"I love you."

"I love you."

He sighed into the phone. "I'll see you Monday night?"

"I'll be there."

The call ended. I watched the flashing call time until the screen turned black, then held it to my chest, moisture finding my eyes. "He sounds so sad."

Grandma rubbed my shoulder. "It's going to be hard. You just need to be there while he works through it."

I nodded, blinking. "I just feel completely helpless."

Her eyes lit up. "Maybe not completely." She pushed the button on her chair, and the leg rest went down, painfully slowly. "We can go to their house, make sure they have some good meals to come home to."

My lips twitched. "You mean it?"

"Marta didn't give me a key to their house for nothing."

Even though it wasn't yet five in the morning, we went to the store and got plenty of groceries and disposable pans. Grandma knew all of their favorite meals, the ingredients.

It made me jealous of all the years she spent as their neighbor. How she must have watched Jon grow from a nervous child, to a middle schooler, into the man I fell in love with. I wished I had been there to see it all.

But I was here now, and I needed to make the most of it.

We grabbed coffee on the way back from the store and spent the entire morning cooking. Marta kept her house clean, so there wasn't much I could do to help with that.

As Grandma finished putting lids on the casseroles, I went upstairs to use the bathroom.

Okay, maybe I didn't need to be up there. I mean, there was a bathroom downstairs. But I wanted to see Jon's room. This place where we sat on beanbag chairs and plotted revenge on some kid who left a mean note on my back.

Maybe, in a way, I owed that kid a thank you. Nothing bonded friends like a common enemy.

I stood in the doorway to Jon's room, a time capsule from this summer. Of afternoons spent lying around, listening to music, holding each other, being quiet as we kissed so his parents wouldn't intrude on our special spot—our special moments.

My eyes landed on something new. A photo of us from this summer on his dresser in a simple black frame. He had his arms wrapped around me. We were laughing. His mom must have snapped it without us knowing.

I stepped in and gently touched the frame, a wonderful memory I didn't know I had frozen in place.

A shuffling noise sounded behind me, and I turned to see Grandma coming down the hallway, a soft smile on her face. "I'm so glad you two started going steady. Such a cute couple."

I cringed. "We're *dating,* Grandma. We're not ninety years old."

She drew herself up and feigned an indignant look. "And neither am I. Seventy-seven years young."

I laughed. "Practically a spring chicken."

She came and wrapped her arm around me. "Come on. I want to catch that antique show. I have my sights set on a new old lamp to go with my couch."

I shook my head. Some habits never died.

We got in her car and went to the community event center where tons of vendors had set up booths with everything from decorative knives to old paintings to ornate jewelry.

I'd never been much of a shopping person—it just reminded me of all the money I didn't have—but seeing all the treasures through Grandma's eyes was fun.

Every piece had a story. This painting was like the one that hung in her great-aunt's dining room. That brooch reminded her of a bad substitute teacher. These leather moccasins were just like the ones she had as a kid, playing outside in the summer heat.

We made it all the way down one row, and she bent over, hands on her knees.

"Grandma, are you okay?" I asked.

She nodded. "Just tired."

Worry filled my chest. Grandma never got tired like this. In fact, she had always outpaced me when we went on walks together. "Let's go to the tables."

I wrapped my arm around her and helped her to the nearest table.

She sat down, rubbing her brow. "That early

morning must have been harder on me than I thought."

I wanted so badly for that to be it that I nodded and went along. "I can go get us some coffee from the concession stand?"

She nodded. "And maybe a candy. My blood sugar might be low."

Grandma wasn't a diabetic, but I nodded and got what she asked for.

We sat and drank and ate until she got her energy back. We went back to browsing the stands, but more slowly this time, with less conversation. I had a feeling we both had plenty of thoughts going through our minds.

Around five, she said, "Come on. Let's get dinner."

We drove across town to one of her favorite restaurants. Just as we got seated, she stood back up and went to an older man I recognized from the Scollers' New Year's party.

"Jorge," she said. "I'm so glad you could come."

CHAPTER FIFTY

THEY SAT on the same side of the booth, and I looked between the two of them, begging with my eyes for Grandma to tell me what on earth was going on.

"I asked Jorge to come out to dinner with us," Grandma said. "We've been seeing each other."

She said it like it was no big deal, but my eyes bugged out. "Seeing each other? Don't you mean 'going steady'?"

Jorge laughed, deep and slow. "Are kids still saying that nowadays?"

Grandma giggled, lighter and more carefree than I'd seen her since Grandpa died. "No. She's teasing me."

I couldn't help but smile. "So I was right?"

She nodded.

Being the third wheel on a surprise date with my grandma was awkward, but I was happy for her. I didn't like the idea of her being alone. And Jorge seemed sweet. Especially when he did all the old-timey gentlemanly things like laying her napkin in her lap and taking the check without even asking.

After dinner, he walked us out to Grandma's car and opened the doors for both of us. He opened Grandma's door last and bent to kiss her on the cheek. She smiled like a schoolgirl.

He leaned over and grinned at me. "Thanks for sharing your grandmother with me. She's quite a gal."

"I agree," I said, a stupid grin on my own face.

After he closed the door, I elbowed Grandma. "Did you hear that. You're *quite a gal.*"

She batted my arm away, hiding a smile. "Oh, stop it."

"Why didn't you tell me you were *going steady* with someone?"

"I thought this would be easier," she said, buckling up. "I thought it might be hard to see me with someone other than your grandpa."

I shook my head and gave her my eyes, telling

her I was serious. "I want you to be happy, Gram. Whatever makes you happy."

Her smile was conflicted. "Sometimes it's not that simple. You mean more to me than any man ever will."

I reached over and hugged her across the console. "I'm so lucky to have you."

She hugged me back with one arm and kissed my cheek, no doubt leaving a red ring of lipstick behind. "Love you, sweetie." She put her car in reverse and started backing out. "Now, tell me what you decided to do—or not do—with Jon."

I cringed. "Grandma, do you *really* want to talk about this with me?"

She shrugged. "I need to know whether to take you to the women's clinic or not."

"I think so." Thankfully, she kept her eyes on the road so she couldn't see how much I was panicking. "But how do I even know if I'm ready?"

Her lips lifted on one side. "You'll just know. And if you love Jon as much as I think you do, I'd rather you be safe than sorry."

CHAPTER FIFTY-ONE

MY PHONE VIBRATED with a call from Stormy, and I picked it up.

"Hey," she said, "you left yet?"

"Nope, getting gas now, though."

"Come by the restaurant. It's dead as hell, and I want to say goodbye."

I wanted to have time to get back, take a shower and quick nap before seeing Jon, but I wanted to see Stormy too. There was never enough of me—or my time—anymore.

"I'll be there in a few."

Stormy was right about the restaurant being dead. The parking lot might as well have had tumble-weeds blowing around for how empty it was. I took a spot right up front and walked inside.

Stormy leaned over the counter, her cheek in one hand and phone in the other. At the sound of the door opening, she perked up.

"Thank God, Abi," she said, walking toward me. "Bored?"

"To death." She hugged me, then waved for me to follow her. "What do you want to drink? Shirley Temple? Hot cocoa? Nothing is too nice—or free—for the godmother of my future child."

"Just tea with lemon," I said. Then. "Wait. What? Godmother?"

She gave me a nervous smile. "If you're up for it?"

I nodded so fast, a loose hair fell in my face and I had to brush it back. "I mean, of course, but are you sure? You don't want Macy or Leanne to do it?"

"No," she said. "I want you to teach my child what it's like to overcome the odds and fight for *exactly* what you want." There was a ferocity in her eyes that told me this hadn't been a spur-of-the-moment decision. She'd chosen me.

There weren't words to tell her how much that meant, so instead I hugged her tight.

She sniffed slightly and turned toward the drink machine. "Iced tea it is."

That was Stormy. She said what needed to be said and didn't dwell in the emotions of it all.

I followed her on the opposite side of the counter like I had all summer and sat in one of the two-person tables. While I was here, there was one thing I could use her advice on...

She walked over and set a sweating glass in front of me. "Any plans for tonight?"

I shook my head and told her about Jon's cousin.

Sympathy transformed her features. "We need to send him a card or something. Can you get me his address?"

I nodded, picked at my thumbnail.

"How are you two doing?"

A slight smile came to my lips. The lips that were permanently and forever Jon's. "We're doing good."

"Okay, you have to tell me. Have you two had sex yet?"

My cheeks reddened as I shook my head. When would I become one of those girls who was cool about sex? Or would that just elude me forever?

"Are you...saving it?"

Saving it. Like sex was something I could stick in my bank account for a rainy day. More like a life-changing, relationship-changing decision that would follow me for all of forever.

"No," I said. "I'm not saving it. Actually..." I stalled and then pulled the slim pack of pills from my purse and showed them to her.

Her eyes widened. "Seriously? Are you ready for that?"

Grandma had said I would know. I knew about Jon. That night spent lying side by side with him was enough to tell me I wanted to lie with him every single night for the rest of forever. How much better would it feel being even closer to Jon?

"I love him so much," I said.

A frown touched her lips for a second. "I wish I would have waited for Frank. He said he didn't mind that I wasn't a virgin, but still..."

"It's now that matters, right? Besides"—I nodded toward her midsection—"you're sharing something with him you've never shared with another guy."

Now she smiled. "That's true." She stalled. "So you're okay that Jon's not a virgin then?"

I'd never been through an earthquake, but this had to be what one felt like. Like the ground that had once been steady was shaking underneath you, and you had no idea when it would stop or even how long it would last or what would get ruined in the process.

What your life would look like after the ground had cracked and everything you held dear fell off the shelves and shattered.

"What?" I managed.

Her eyes went wide. "You didn't know?"

I could only get one word out. One name. "Denise?"

Remorsefully, Stormy nodded.

She shouldn't have been apologetic. She wasn't the one who had sex with Jon's ex-girlfriend and kept it a secret. She was just the one who told me the heartbreaking news.

Here I'd thought we were on level playing field. That when Jon's mom talked about waiting until marriage it would be *our* marriage he'd be pretending to wait for.

Why hadn't he told me?

How could I tell him I knew?

CHAPTER FIFTY-TWO

ROAD HYPNOSIS: when you're driving and you go into a hypnotic state. Your brain goes on autopilot, getting you home safely without much conscious thought.

I didn't know how, but I made it back to Austin. To the college. To the crowded parking lot and up the stairs.

Until I reached the dorm and found Anika on her bed, watching something on her laptop. Then my eyes latched onto a new note on my desk.

I snapped back to reality. Back to *my* reality.

Where the only person who put me first was the creep writing me letters and my problems were too big to tug people from their busy lives.

She smiled at me, and I became the actress my

abusive parents had trained me to be. I smiled back and said, "Hey, how was your weekend?"

She popped out an earbud. "It was amazing. So needed. What about you?"

"Same. It was good to see my friends."

"Did you get some time with Jon?"

I frowned. "No, his cousin was in the hospital and died this weekend. It's been really hard on him."

"Poor guy," she said, her expression somber. "I'll be praying for him, and I'll give Kyle a head's up."

"Thanks." I tried to sound grateful, but honestly, I was just wiped. Whatever reserves I had left, I'd just used trying to pretend like everything was okay.

"You look exhausted," she said.

I nodded, thankful for the out. "I am. I think I'm going to shower and get some sleep before he gets here."

"Sure," she said and put her earbud back in. Conversation over.

I grabbed a new outfit, my shower caddy, and a towel and went to the community showers. I'd forgotten my shower shoes, but at this point, I had bigger things to worry about.

The hot water pounded against the yellowish tile, and I stepped underneath the stream. Showers used to relax me, but now the relentless water felt like just one more thing trying to drown me.

Giving up, I twisted my wet hair into a ratty knot, shrugged on my outfit consisting of sweatpants and a T-shirt, and shuffled back to our room.

Anika gave me a concerned look but didn't pry.

That made me like her even more.

I dropped my shower caddy on my desk, letting droplets spill onto the unopened letter, and climbed into my bed. Once I'd curled under the covers, I closed my eyes and let sleep utterly and totally consume me.

When I woke up, it was two in the morning, and Jon was lying in the bed with me.

He had his arm draped over my side and his legs curled against mine. It should have felt amazing, but instead I felt trapped. He was a stranger now.

I lifted my head up to see Anika's bed empty. She and Jon must have switched.

I looked down at Jon, his smooth skin and rough five o'clock shadow. The even planes of his face that seemed so relaxed in sleep.

But even that couldn't distract me from seeing all the ways Denise had loved him. All the ways I hadn't. Her hands had brushed his jawline. Her lips had pressed against his. Her *body* had moved against his, in the most intimate of ways.

I had to get off the bed. Had to get away from him and from the ghost of *her*.

So I did. I climbed down the ladder, careful not to wake him, and stuffed my hand in my mouth to keep my sobs from leaking out.

How had we gotten here? How had Jon gone from the love of my life to the love of someone else's?

The stress and worry of it all crushed down on me. So hard I couldn't imagine having room for me and my worry and Jon in an extra-long twin.

Instead, I got into Anika's bed. Slept under her comforter. Because whether I was sleeping underneath her unfamiliar bedding or sleeping in my bed next to Jon, I'd be lying with the unknown.

* * *

"Abi." Jon's husky morning voice woke me.

I blinked my eyes open to see him standing next to the bed.

Our room looked different. Backwards. And then I realized I hadn't slept through a nightmare; I'd woken up to one.

"What are you doing in Anika's bed?" he asked.

His green eyes were worried, pale in the wan morning light.

I shook my head and answered honestly. "I don't know."

"Can you come back to your bed?" He gripped his other arm, and before he looked down, I recognized the look on his face. Fear. Insecurity. Hurt.

I'd put that there. The death of his cousin had put that there. And I couldn't add any more pressure, whether he'd kept secrets from me or not.

I had my fair share of skeletons too. I had to live with mine. And his.

CHAPTER FIFTY-THREE

I BARELY MADE it to practice the next day. Barely survived it, too.

A deep weariness had settled into my bones. Made it hard to do anything other than go to class and practice and sleep. Jon was so lost in his own grief, he didn't seem to notice.

He threw himself into his studies. Into his classes. When he had time, he came to my room. He slept in my bed a lot, but we didn't fool around or even share more than quick, chaste kisses.

I had a feeling he just needed me there, which was good, because that was about all I could do.

At our latest track practice, Nikki had had enough.

"What is going on with you?" she demanded in

the locker room, staring up at me with her hands on her hips. Which I was just tired enough to find funny since I was a good eight inches taller than her.

I turned away to hide my ludicrous smile and got my shirt out of my locker. "I don't know."

She grabbed my wrist and turned me back to her. "Seriously. I'm worried. I never see you in the cafeteria. You're dragging in practice. You have circles under your eyes the size of frisbees. What is going on? Is it about the letters?"

"Shh!" I said, looking around the locker room. No one seemed to have heard us or cared, but I still talked in a hushed tone. "It's not about any of that. My boyfriend's cousin died, and it's hard. And my profs are burying me in homework. I miss my grandma, and my friends, and...it's hard!" I cried, letting all my frustration out on her.

She blinked. "Oh."

"Yeah, oh." I threw my shirt back in my locker and slammed the door shut. "Thanks for the 'concern.'" I shoved past her.

I knew I was being unreasonable. That she was just being a good friend and looking out for me. But that was the thing. I didn't need anyone looking out for me. I'd dealt just fine on my own for my entire life. The last thing I needed was another mom. I had one, and she was Satan incarnate.

Instead of going to dinner like I usually did, I went straight to my dorm and poured all of my frustrations into my homework. I wouldn't let my grades slip. Or my athletics. They were all I had left.

Every time I looked at Jon, I saw the secret. If we ever had sex, he would just realize how much better he could do, and that would be it. There was no winning. Not in my life.

I went to bed after finishing my homework since we had practice at five the next morning. Both of the distance teams were finally going out of town and doing a huge loop Jon had shown me before school started.

The next morning, when I got to the parking lot where everyone was piling into university vans, I caught sight of Jon.

He walked over to me. "I was going to walk with you, but I couldn't get ahold of you last night. Are you okay?"

I rubbed at my tired eyes. "Just exhausted. Whose idea was it to get up this early?"

Coach Cadence cleared her throat. "That would be mine. In the vans, Johnson, Scoller."

We did as told and went to our separate vans. I

got a seat by the window and sat quietly while the cityscape turned to country. There weren't any obvious markers, but Coach Cadence drove like she'd been here a million times before.

She parked alongside the road, and we got out of the van, congregating in the middle of a dirt road. Even though it was before six in the morning, the sun was hot.

I wondered when the fall chill would take over, because I was already sweating. I peeled off my sweater and tossed it back in the van.

"Line up here," Coach Cadence ordered.

I stood at the imaginary line with the other girls. Out of the corner of my eye, I caught sight of Jon with his teammates. Grieving Jon was gone and had been replaced with the determined athlete I'd watched and run alongside in high school.

My heart ached. I loved him. Wanted him.

Maybe he hadn't kept a secret. We hadn't actually talked about it. It wasn't like he'd lied to me or anything.

"Ready," Coach Cadence said.

I shook my head, trying to clear off the groggy, foggy thoughts.

"Set," she continued. "Go!"

We started off as she yelled behind us, "Turn right at the next road!"

As my feet settled into a steady rhythm, I realized how different our surroundings looked than when Jon showed me this area on move-in day. All around us, green stalks shot into the air, dark leaves draping off the shoots, taller than ever before. The dirt road seemed to stretch out before us, no break in the crops in sight.

Soon, though, it took more and more effort to keep up with the other girls. Before we even reached the first turn, I fell to the back of the team. Soon, I was yards behind them. At least a hundred.

If I was being honest, this wasn't anything new. The last couple of weeks had been hard, making my averages slow. I was even further from belonging on the team than I had been when I started. Shame made me want to push myself to catch up with them, but I worried I wouldn't be able to finish if I kept at their pace.

Nikki dropped back beside me and huffed, "You can do this, Abi. Push."

She was right. I'd been through hell and back. Done all the same workouts as the others. I could keep up with my team.

I fought like I'd fought the year before. For my

grades. For my weight. For my mile time. Every part of me longed to feel like I had earned a place on the team and that I wouldn't just be another college dropout.

"That's it!" she yelled.

My mind flashed back to that good feeling when I ran my second timed mile with Jon running beside me. He'd encouraged me. Helped me be my best. I wanted to be that girl again.

But my legs gave out below me, and everything went black.

CHAPTER FIFTY-FOUR

I LAY in the training room on one of four exam tables, staring at the florescent lights. One was burnt out. A moth fluttered in front of the other one.

The team's athletic trainer had just left after bandaging my legs and shoulders. He'd cleaned out countless flecks of gravel and broken-off stickers, covering the wounds with stinging antiseptic before wrapping them with gauze. My entire body felt like an open wound, pulsating with every beat of my heart.

He said the physician would be coming in to do a full exam, including blood work, at which point I should be able to get some painkillers.

No matter how much I wanted them, I knew I'd never take more than acetaminophen or ibuprofen. I'd never go down the same path as my parents.

The moth in the lights slowed to a stop, and its dark outline added to the insect graveyard hanging over my head.

Gross.

I sighed. I thought one of the perks of being an athlete was getting special treatment. I didn't know I'd still have to wait around forever for a doctor.

To be fair, it was only half past seven in the morning.

I wished I had my phone to keep my mind busy. Even a textbook or homework assignment would be better than sitting here letting my brain wander. What did I do before I had a phone with data?

Oh yeah, books.

But I didn't have any of those tucked in my sweatpants.

I stared at a diagram of the human body framed on the wall, reading each muscle and vein on the poster, not really taking any of it in.

There were muffled voices outside the door. They got louder, almost like an argument. But then the yelling stalled, and a man walked in. He didn't have a white coat on like I'd expected, but a stethoscope hung around his neck.

"Abigail?" he said.

"Abi."

"Right." His eyes scanned the clipboard in his hand like that information was more important than the body right in front of him. "Tell me what happened."

I rolled my eyes back toward the light, not bothering to get up. "I was running and then I passed out."

"What do you think caused it?"

I shrugged, paper crackling beneath me. "I thought that's why they called you in."

He snorted softly. "Well, let's give you a listen."

I breathed as instructed while the stethoscope moved over my body.

"All clear," he said.

I'd known it would be.

The wheels of a rolling chair scraped over the tile, and the cushion whooshed as he sat down. "Okay, let's do some detective work."

I was silent.

"Did you eat this morning?"

"Before five a.m.? No."

"And did you drink alcohol last night?" he grilled.

"No."

"What about this weekend? You won't get in trouble."

"No."

"Have you been fatigued?" he asked.

"Yeah."

"How often?"

"You pick," I said. "College is hard."

"It is," he agreed, his pen scratching over paper. "What did you have for supper last night?"

I closed my eyes, knowing my answer wouldn't sound good. "Nothing."

More writing.

"Have a big lunch?"

"No."

"Breakfast?"

"No."

"Abigail," he said. "Are you telling me you haven't eaten for more than twenty-four hours?"

"It's been a hard week," I managed.

"A week?" He barely kept the surprise out of his voice. "How long has it been since you've had a decent meal?"

I kept my eyes closed, wishing I could block out his question. I knew the answer. It was when Nikki had forced me to eat all that stir-fry more than two weeks ago. I'd just gotten by since then, opting for sleep over food until my stomach growled so loudly I couldn't ignore it. "A week. Maybe?"

He sighed the emotionally tired way older people often did. "Look at me." When I rolled my head over, I was met by caring hazel eyes. "I'm going to refer you to the campus psychiatrist, and I'm calling in the team nutritionist. If you want to have any future in Upton athletics, you need to do as they say."

He stood up and turned toward the door. "Oh, and there are people here to see you. I had them wait until we were finished."

My brow creased. People?

When he opened the door, Jon and Nikki immediately rushed in, still wearing their practice uniforms.

Jon gingerly took my uninjured cheek in his hand, his eyes searching every inch of my body. "Are you okay?"

I nodded and folded my arms over my stomach.

He settled onto the exam table beside me, warmth leaking through his clothes and heating my body. "They said you just collapsed."

Nikki stood off to the side, her arms crossed over her chest. "She did. It was terrifying."

"I must have just been tired," I lied.

Jon and Nikki exchanged a look, leaving me on the defensive.

"What?" I asked.

Jon nodded at Nikki. "She said you haven't been eating. That practice has been like this for weeks." His eyes still roved every inch of my face. "What have you done, Abi?"

CHAPTER FIFTY-FIVE

I STARED at the two of them, torn between being ashamed and feeling angry.

How had Nikki violated my privacy in such a huge way? If I'd wanted Jon to know, I would have told him. What was Jon accusing me of, anyway? Caring for him more than myself?

But even as I thought those words, I knew my actions had gone too far for too long. I stared down at my hands, at my wrists that for the first time had clearly defined bones. I wasn't emaciated by any stretch of the word, but I wasn't healthy either.

As Jon had asked, what had I done?

Jon didn't leave me time to answer his question, instead saying, "Nikki told me about the notes."

I gaped at her. Now I was mad. Why had she

worried him with something I'd wanted to keep to myself? He had enough to worry about, much less me and letters we could do nothing about. This stressed look on his face with deep lines and creased corners was exactly what I had been trying to avoid.

"Have you told the cops?" he demanded.

"We did," Nikki spoke up, but at my glare, she quieted.

"They blew it off," I said. "There's nothing they could do, and I didn't want to worry you."

"Well, I am worried," he said, more angry than concerned. "You've been so stressed about it you've stopped eating! Why have you been doing this to yourself?"

"I—" My dry throat kept me from finishing. I swallowed and looked down at my hands. They looked like a stranger's. "I just got caught up in it all."

"Not good enough," he said, livid. "I need an answer. A real one."

Somehow, I managed to bring my eyes up to his. "I did it for you."

The horror that crossed his face was so much more pronounced than the worry before. He swayed on the table, and he gripped the edge of it to steady himself. "What do you mean you did this for me?"

He gestured at me. "What made you think I ever wanted *this*?"

Every one of my cracks separated from the gold, if there ever was any. I had to make him understand. "I was just some charity case Coach Cadence took on to get you. I wanted to earn my place here. To earn you."

His jaw worked, and he wouldn't even meet my eyes. "I'm not a trophy you can earn. I wanted to be with you—fat, skinny, couch potato, college athlete— I didn't care! Everything I loved about you was already there. Don't you understand that?"

"No!" I cried, barely noticing Nikki shying away from us. "Of course I don't understand it! Look at you! You're attractive, athletic, smart, kind. You could get any girl you want, and you choose me? Of course it doesn't make sense!"

"Are we here again?" he asked, exasperated. "Abi, how can I get it through to you that I think you're amazing? What other people have done to you has *nothing* to do with how I feel about you."

"But what about what I've done?" I asked. "Or haven't done?"

His eyes seemed to go darker, like he had caught on to what I was referring to. "What do you mean?"

I bit my lip, shook my head, unable to say it out

loud. "I just don't know how to reconcile this. Us. How did I end up with you?"

He raked his hands through his hair. "You have got to take me off that pedestal, Abi. I can't live up to that guy you're saying I am."

"I can't live up to the girl who deserves him."

"Then I have nothing more to say." He stood up and started walking away.

I sat up, leaning toward him. "What are you saying?"

"I'm saying it's over." He turned and continued walking away. "I can't be the reason you hurt yourself. Not anymore."

CHAPTER FIFTY-SIX

THE NUTRITIONIST CAME in after Jon left, but I wasn't there. Not mentally, at least.

I was in the moment where Jon had said it was over and walked away.

At the worst moment of my life.

At the moment where I ruined everything that mattered to me.

So when she scheduled regular counseling appointments for me, I nodded. When she told me one of her graduate assistants would be meeting me at every meal and spending the following hour after with me to make sure I wouldn't purge, I shrugged.

She said it was that or get kicked off the team.

Like that was any consequence.

I'd already lost everything that mattered to me.

Running around in a circle for a college education was the least of my worries.

Some kid who looked only a few years older than me came into the training room and took a sheet from *Deborah*. A meal plan with a list of things to eat.

"In the meantime," she said, "eat this." She handed me a protein bar.

With unfeeling fingers, I shoved the cardboard-tasting food in my mouth and chewed. It was all I could do to keep from gagging. From the food or from the heartache, I didn't know.

The guy, the graduate assistant, started walking toward the door, and when he stalled, I realized he was expecting me to follow him.

Somehow, I made my legs move. They should have been weak and shaky, but I couldn't feel anything except the gaping hole in my chest where Jon used to occupy my heart.

I'd done everything I could to keep him, and I still managed to screw it up.

Just like I'd messed up with my parents. They didn't love me for a reason. Chose life-ruining drugs over their own daughter. I should have been used to not being enough by now, but it hurt even worse coming from Jon.

I didn't even care what I looked like walking into the dining hall with some guy I barely knew choosing my food and carrying my plate for me. Or that he watched my every move like I was dangerous.

Maybe I was.

To myself, at least.

I worked my way through eggs, sausage, sweet potatoes, and cottage cheese until my stomach felt like it would burst.

"I can't eat anymore," I said.

"That's fine," the guy said. I still hadn't asked his name. He hadn't offered it. "I can wait until it digests a little."

He said it in that falsely cheery way people talked to me when my parents were getting hauled off to prison and photos were being taken of my mangled face. Like everything would be okay.

It clearly wouldn't.

We sat there for the better part of two hours. He at least had the decency not to make any more conversation. I didn't offer to talk, instead scrolling through my phone. I'd grabbed it when we picked up my backpack on the way here, looking for something, anything to distract me from this pain that just kept growing, threatening to crush my lungs.

I inevitably made it to Jon's social media

accounts. His profile picture had changed from one of us at prom to one of him at graduation. By himself. My name wasn't on his relationship status. It had been hidden.

I covered my mouth. Just when I thought the hole in my chest couldn't grow any larger, it threatened to swallow me whole.

"Are you okay?" the guy asked, his voice speeding. "Do you feel sick? Do I need to get you a bucket?"

I couldn't even bring myself to unglue my eyes from the screen long enough to tell him to stop running for a cup.

When I finally managed to break my gaze away, he was talking to someone behind the serving line, gesturing wildly.

I made a run for it. I didn't know where or why, but I left the dining hall as fast as I could. With the doors closing behind me, I dialed the only numbers I could think of in my phone.

Eric picked up. "Hey, beautiful, what are you doing?"

"Come pick me up," I said, barely masking my hysteria. "Now."

"Is everything okay?"

The grad assistant's voice yelled behind me.

"Come pick me up," I repeated, my voice rising. "The dorm parking lot. Now."

"I'll be there," he said and hung up.

I gripped my phone tightly in my hand and ran. I needed to get as far away from here, from my feelings, as I possibly could.

CHAPTER FIFTY-SEVEN

A PICKUP PULLED ALONGSIDE ME, and Eric yelled my name out the window.

I ran to the passenger side and yanked the door open.

"What's wrong?" he asked, concern plain on his face. "Are you hurt?"

"Get me out of here." I threw my backpack inside, climbed in, and slammed the door behind me. "Anywhere."

While he drove, I curled into the passenger seat and cried until I couldn't cry anymore. Until some combination of the heavy food in my stomach and the weight on my heart dragged me into dark sleep shrouded with shadowy figures.

When I blearily blinked my eyes open, Eric was

still driving, his fingers thrumming on the steering wheel.

I pushed myself up, looking at the pastures flying past our windows. At the dust billowing behind us. At the hazy sky. How long had I been asleep?

"Where are we?" I asked.

"A little north of the border," he said, staring straight ahead, expressionless.

"The border?" My mind was still fuzzy from the sleep and the food and the day. "Which one?"

"Mexico," he said.

My brows came together. "What are we doing here?"

His lips quirked, but no humor lit his eyes. "You said to take you anywhere. I thought I'd show you the family ranch."

I shifted in my seat, feeling little unsettled. "Why's that?"

He shrugged. "It was about as far away from the college as I could think."

As far away from Jon.

I sat back in my seat, trying to make myself stay calm. His dash clock said one o'clock. I knew that couldn't be right. When I looked for my phone to see what time it was, I couldn't find it. I looked through my backpack, even checking the small front pocket, but I must have lost it in my race to get away from the cafeteria.

All I found there was Eric's number from the first day of class. Something about the note looked eerily familiar—

"What are you looking for?" he asked.

"Nothing," I answered, too quickly. "Are we almost there?"

"Almost," he said.

"Will we make it back to the college by morning?"

He shrugged. "You might miss a few classes. Seemed like you had bigger things to worry about when you called me and cried yourself to sleep."

He was right. Missing a few classes wouldn't be the end of the world. I'd probably get kicked off the track team, but at this point, I couldn't care less. I could go home to Grandma and lick my wounds. Tell her college hadn't panned out. Get a job at the restaurant with Stormy now that the Scollers wouldn't want anything to do with me.

Besides, I needed the distraction from Jon. The way he'd looked at me.

We rode in silence for another hour until he turned onto a trail off the road. I tried to make out our surroundings, but it was so dark here, like in the country by Denison Cemetery. The vehicle rattled over a metal grate in the ground, and then he took his pickup on a well-traveled dirt path, rutted into the scrubby pasture.

"Is this the way to your house?" I asked.

"No," he said. "I wanted to show you something else first."

I looked around us, trying to make out any landmarks in the black landscape, but I couldn't see much except lights of various sizes and colors in the distance.

He parked and killed the headlights, bathing us in total darkness.

I looked over to his features outlined in pale silver light. He would have been handsome to me in another life. One where I hadn't met and been ruined by Jon Scoller.

He turned his gaze on me. It seemed flat. "Do you see that line of lights up there?"

I nodded.

"It's a feedlot," he explained. "Most of the ranchers around here send their cattle there to fatten them up. At night, a lot of people meet the dealers there from across the border to get drugs."

Ice water dripped through my veins at the mention of drugs. I tried not to show just how much that word impacted me. Shook me to my core. So I just nodded.

"They leave us alone, and we leave them alone. It's just part of life by the border. I used to take my girlfriend—Lupita—out there at night to watch our cattle. We'd sit in the view box overlooking the lot and talk about our future. Her dad has a ranch just like mine does. We were going to merge our properties one day. Become one of the biggest operations in southwest Texas."

Why was he talking about her in the past tense? He'd never told me about her. "Where is she now?" I asked.

His lips curled downward, and he rubbed his brows. "We were going out there one night, and there were police lights everywhere. They'd decided to bust them. This SUV came flying toward us, trying to outrun the cops, and clipped our front end. He kept going, but we caught the drop-off on the road and went flying."

A mental picture flooded my mind of Dad coming home after one of his stints away, our SUV with a damaged front end sitting in front of the house. He told Mom he'd driven into a fence. It couldn't have been him. There were plenty of SUVs in the world.

"My pickup rolled. Eight times. She was sitting by me in the middle seat. Wasn't buckled up."

I covered my mouth, stifling the urge to vomit.

"She flew through the window. The pickup crushed her, Abi. I found her, twenty yards off. I couldn't even recognize her through all the blood, the *meat*."

I gagged.

"She was dead before I even got to her. I didn't get to say goodbye."

My eyes watered, while my throat stayed so dry I couldn't even utter a worthless apology.

"I swore I'd find the piece of shit who did it. Make them pay for what they took from me. From Lupita and her family and our future." He stared at the lights, his face twisted. "So I went back, every night, waiting for that SUV. And it came back. I followed it, all the way through Texas. Back to some shithole town.

"And I found exactly what I could take from him to make him feel even a little bit of the pain he caused me." His eyes met mine, dark black and dead inside. "You."

CHAPTER FIFTY-EIGHT

HE LUNGED FOR ME, but I reached for the door handle and scrambled out of the pickup. I fell onto the uneven ground, my hands scraping over rough weeds and cacti.

I got my footing under me and ran, as fast as I could, as hard as I could, plucking spines from my hands.

"GET BACK HERE, ABI!" Eric bellowed behind me. "WE'RE NOT FINISHED!"

There was no time to think, to respond, only adrenaline flowing and arms pumping and legs burning to carry me as far away as possible.

Footsteps pounded behind me, but I'd gotten a head start. I was fast. And the meal earlier combined with adrenaline rushing through my body gave me the energy I needed to outrun him. Or die trying.

The footsteps stopped, but I didn't give up, still racing as fast as I could. I didn't trust my ears or anything other than my legs moving and moving until I was away from the monster I'd thought was my friend.

The ground was uneven, but my eyes had adjusted to the darkness, going hyper-alert. I made sure to dodge the taller scrub bushes, the holes that randomly peppered the ground.

An engine roared to life, Eric's, and headlights flooded the pasture in front of me, blinding me.

I raced down the hillside, panic rising up in my throat. I couldn't outrun a pickup, not out here, and not forever.

A gully at least five feet deep appeared in front of me, and I leapt over it. It wasn't far enough. I scrabbled on the edge and pulled myself up. My survival depended on it.

The horn honked loudly, repeatedly, and a little bit of me gave up inside, knowing there was no one near enough to hear what was happening. To save me.

The earth in front of me started rising, but I knew going up a hill would just slow me down. I ran alongside the gully, clods of dirt dropping to the bottom and busting open.

Tires spun against dirt behind me. He'd gone around the drop-off and was driving along the hillside, coming closer and closer.

I chanced a glance back and caught sight of his arm sticking out the driver's side window, a gun in his grasp.

My heart stopped. Stalled. Gave out.

But my legs kept working.

I couldn't outrun a bullet any more than I could a pickup.

It fired off, the roar of the gun ringing in my ears.

I waited for pain, but none came.

He'd missed.

Two more shots fired, but neither of them hit me either.

Then came the sound of crunching metal, the headlights spewing all over the countryside, turning and making me dizzy.

I chanced a look back. The hill had gotten too steep, and the pickup was rolling, down into the gully.

My foot caught on a scrub bush, and I tumbled to the ground, scraping my already wounded cheek against hard earth. I got up just in time to see the pickup come to its final stop, lying on its side in the middle of the gully, headlights pointed straight ahead.

For some strange, sadistic, masochistic reason, my heart went to the man inside the pickup. But I couldn't let my thoughts stay there if I wanted to keep my life.

So I ran. I ran with tears streaking down my eyes. I ran until every single breath burned and my feet ached, begging me to stop.

I ran until the floodlights of a simple country home came into view and I reached the front door, banging frantically.

A Hispanic woman in nightwear and her husband came to the door, their eyes squinted against the newly lit lights in their home.

In a fraction of a second, their expressions fired from drowsy to shocked.

Exhausted, ragged, bleeding, I couldn't manage more than a gasp. "Help."

CHAPTER FIFTY-NINE

THEY SPOKE to each other in hurried Spanish as the man hooked his arms under my elbows and brought me inside to their kitchen.

She shoved the chairs aside, and he lowered me to the floor, still speaking in Spanish. Giving orders, I realized, as his wife left, returning with wet rags and a brown bottle.

"*Que pasó?*" he asked, his accent thick.

"What?" I muttered, eyes darting from him to the hands fumbling with the brown bottle.

"What happened?" he asked with a heavy accent.

The woman whispered, "Be painful," and then splashed peroxide over my arm. I cried out as she began plucking what looked like cactus spines from my skin.

My words ached against my throat as I gritted them out. "He tried to kill me."

"¡*Alguien trató matarla!*" the man said.

His wife gasped.

"Where?" he demanded, standing up and going to the doorway. To the shotgun that leaned against the coatrack.

I managed to point in the direction I'd run from. "He wrecked. A white pickup."

His eyes went wide, and he said, "*Llama a la policia. Y a los Shepherds.*"

I recognized Eric's last name.

They knew him. His pickup.

The door slammed behind him, and the woman left me to go to the phone. She spoke in hurried Spanish before hanging up.

"Cops be here soon," she managed, carefully picking each word. She held the phone out to me. "You call?"

I reached for it, my fingers going to the keys, pressing out the numbers that were more familiar than my own.

"This is Jon," he answered.

And at the sound of his voice, I broke down into sobs.

CHAPTER SIXTY

THE POLICE CAME to the house. They brought paramedics with them who picked up where the woman left off.

I still didn't know her name.

They spoke to her in Spanish, and then one of the officers left.

An older man crouched in front of me on the kitchen floor, then sat down cross-legged like he hadn't been lower than a chair in twenty years.

He wrapped his arms around his knees and laced his fingers together. "You've been through a lot tonight."

I nodded.

"And it's not over." His voice was firm, urgent. "I need you to tell me what happened."

As I repeated the nightmare I was still living, my voice didn't even sound like it belonged to me. It was impassive, numb, stating gory details that would horrify another person as appalling facts.

But I'd been through pain before. I'd tried to run away. I'd suffered beatings, wondering if it would go on until I died. I'd been through police interrogations.

There had just never been a gun.

The enemy had never been someone I trusted on my own volition.

Never someone unrelated.

The only part of me that felt anything was the part that held on to Jon. I'd managed to tell him I was somewhere in Texas. That the cops were coming. That I loved him.

When the lights flashed outside, the woman took the phone from me.

He still didn't know where I was.

But he'd made me a promise. "I'm coming."

The cop tore my thoughts away from Jon. "Do you have any questions for me?"

"Where am I?"

"You're about an hour southeast of El Paso."

The door to the house opened, and two people

who looked to be hastily dressed walked in. They immediately went to the officer.

"Sheriff Anderson. Where's Eric?" the woman demanded while the man looked around the house. At me.

He had Eric's wavy hair, though it was thinning at the top. And his chin.

I cringed away from him.

The Hispanic woman noticed and pulled me into her, protecting me from him.

"What's going on?" the man said harshly.

The sheriff answered, "We have reason to believe your son attacked this young lady as revenge for Lupita's death."

The woman who had to be Eric's mom covered her mouth and sagged into her husband. "No."

"He wrecked his vehicle in the pasture south of here. We have officers searching for him now."

"Is he alive?" she asked.

"We don't know."

She came closer to me, yelling, "What did you do to him?"

Her husband held her back, but that didn't stop her words. "Eric would never hurt anyone! WHAT DID YOU DO TO HIM?"

The woman holding me stood up, positioning her petite body between me and Eric's mom, pointing at the door. "OUT!"

She didn't have more words in English, but she didn't need them. The officer herded them outside where there was more yelling. More *wailing*.

Soon, lights flashed, and Eric's parents disappeared. I still couldn't get them out of my mind. Eric's face when he'd said he knew what to take from my dad.

Eric had everything. Parents who cared. A true love. A job and a path to a degree. A future to come home to. And he'd wasted it trying to get back at a man who couldn't care less about me.

A few knocks sounded on the door, and a woman walked in. She looked...normal. Too normal for the situation, dressed in jeans and a plain T-shirt, a cardigan wrapped tightly around her.

Her eyes were sharp as they met mine, and then she went to the Hispanic woman who still paced the kitchen, guarding me like I was her own daughter.

My heart ached for her loss. I didn't think I could feel any more hatred toward my parents, but what I felt for my dad went beyond that. I despised him for doing this to them.

And for what? Another fix? Some extra cash he would just use on more drugs?

It disgusted me in every possible sense of the word. His web had stretched far beyond my bruises. Beyond our family. How many people had been affected by the drugs he and Mom used, bought and sold? How many families?

The woman with sharp eyes came and crouched in front of me. My protector let her by, so I immediately trusted her.

"Abigail," she said. "I'm with the El Paso PD. The sheriff thought you might be more comfortable staying with me instead of at the jail until arrangements can be made to get you home."

I looked between her and the other woman, nodded.

"Follow me." She started toward the door, and I trailed behind her. I didn't have anything to bring with me.

I was about to shut the door behind me when I looked back and saw my self-appointed caretaker standing in the kitchen. In the last few hours, she'd been more of a rescuer—more of a mom—than mine had ever been.

"What's your name?" I asked.

"Mireya," she said.

"Thank you, Mireya." I stalled. "For everything."

My words would never be enough, but they were all I had.

CHAPTER SIXTY-ONE

THE COP, Sheila, let me sit in the front seat of her patrol car. She waited for me to get belted in before driving down the dirt road, headlights illuminating the path ahead.

I sank low in my seat, remembering the sounds of gunshots behind me.

I could be dead in the middle of a pasture right now, but instead, I'd escaped. I never could have done that when I'd weighed more than two hundred pounds. But I couldn't have done it this morning either.

I needed to treat my body better. Like the useful, life-saving tool it had been for me. Not something designed to earn respect or affection. Jon had done what he had to for my protection, but the truth was, it was never his fault. I'd tortured myself all on my own, holding on to fabricated evidence that told me I didn't deserve any good in life.

"Do you have questions?" Sheila asked.

I dragged myself away from my thoughts. "When...how am I getting home?"

"We will make calls tonight to get you back. We have the resources to drive you there if needed."

I nodded. "How soon will we leave?"

"As soon as we know the plan."

Now that I'd escaped, I wanted to get back to the safety of Woodman as soon as possible. To tell Jon how wrong I'd been. To thank Nikki for caring for me like I should have been caring for myself. To hold my grandma tighter than I ever had before.

"How far is your house?" I asked.

"Another ten minutes."

I waited, my body still strung tighter than a guitar string ready to break. Adrenaline was slowly dissipating from my system, leaving only pain behind. The morning would be rough, but nothing compared to what I'd been through.

She parked in front of a simple stucco home with a one-car garage. My eyes darted around us on the way to the front door to see if anyone was watching.

At least we seemed to be alone.

She let me inside and flipped on the lights, revealing a warmly decorated living room. Somewhere deep inside me wondered whether she regularly brought people here. *Victims* here.

"This is the living room," she said, locking the door behind her. When both deadbolts were secured, she started through the room, indicating I should follow her.

She showed me the kitchen, where the food was, the bathroom, her room, and the guest room. We stood inside the latter together as she retrieved extra blankets and some generic sweats from the dresser that told me she certainly had done this before.

Then she showed me the windows—the locks on them.

"You are safe here," she reassured, meeting my eyes. "I know it will be hard to sleep after everything you've been through, but you are safe. I will be awake in the living room all night, looking out for you."

My eyes watered as that word—safe—echoed in my mind.

"You must be starving," she said. "I'll bring you some food."

My chest constricted the second she closed the door behind her. I busied myself changing out of my track clothes that were still stained with blood and dirt. I hoped the athletic department would be okay with the damage, then realized I was ridiculous for thinking of that in a time like this.

Sheila came back in, bringing a tray of food and drink options, and then left me to myself. I wasn't hungry at first, but I forced myself to eat—to do what I knew was good for me. When the food passed my lips, I became ravenous, eating and drinking until every bit was gone.

My eyelids got heavy, and I fell asleep, dreaming of all I would say when I finally saw Jon.

CHAPTER SIXTY-TWO

MY DREAMS BECAME SO REAL, it almost felt like Jon was lying in bed next to me, holding me tight and cocooning me from the world. I needed him—his protection and warmth. His love.

Dream Abi relaxed into him, letting Jon cradle her.

Real Abi blinked her eyes open and realized she hadn't been dreaming at all.

I sat bolt upright in the bed, and Jon rose behind me. He was fully dressed, in jeans and a T-shirt, his tennis shoes still on his feet. My heart clung to him, something familiar in this unfamiliar space—unfamiliar situation.

He moved to sit beside me, his hand on my back.

I felt every single one of his fingers, the comforting pressure soothing my aching body.

"What are you doing here?" I asked.

He gripped my unbandaged fingers while his other hand tenderly held my face. "I could ask you the same thing."

My lips twitched, but quickly fell. "I'm so sorry."

Shushing me, he pulled me into a hug. "I'm sorry. You wouldn't have been here if it weren't for me."

I shook my head, nearing sobs. "I just wanted to get away from campus. I never thought it would lead to...this." I shuddered at the memories of last night, fresher and more painful than any nightmare.

"You thought you had a friend," he said. "It's not your fault."

"It was though. If I hadn't been so stupid about the letters and track and my weight, and—"

"It's my fault," he insisted.

"You didn't do anything wrong," I said into his shoulder.

"I did. I made you feel like you weren't enough. I should have told you every day how amazing you are. I should have taken my chance before you lost the weight."

My heart tightened at his words. I wanted to argue, but part of me had always wondered if he'd finally decided to date me only because I'd become thin.

"I knew I had to meet you the second I saw you on the bus. I knew I wanted to date you when I walked into my dining room and saw you sitting there. And I knew I couldn't live without you the second I walked away from you this morning."

The shards of my heart slowly came back together. "But..."

"No buts," he said. Then he pulled back and looked in my eyes, caught my heart with the emotion I saw behind the most beautiful green. "Everything I loved about you was already there. You never had to be anything more than Abi. Your family problems, your weight, your mile time—none of that changed my mind about you. Abi was *always* enough."

I held on to him, for the first time believing every single word.

CHAPTER SIXTY-THREE

NOW THAT JON WAS HERE, I couldn't imagine staying another second in Sheila's house.

She said she understood, but we still had to go to the police station for my official statement. Jon went with me, refusing to leave my side.

He didn't flinch away from my account of the day. Instead, he held my hand tighter, his jaw tightening with each detail.

"What's happening to this guy?" he demanded of the investigator.

She shook her head. "If he survives, the case will go to trial."

"If he survives?" Jon asked.

"He is in critical condition," she said. "He's lucky he made it."

I covered my mouth in horror.

Jon gritted his teeth together. "Lucky?"

She looked between Jon and me. "I'll give you two a minute."

With the door shut behind her, Jon stood, fuming, "I hope he suffers. He should die a thousand times over for what he put you through. What he was planning to do to you."

I cringed, knowing there was a real possibility I could have been dead in the pasture. Tortured slowly by someone who wanted nothing more than to transfer his pain to me. Not sitting here beside Jon.

"I can't help but feel responsible, though," I said. "He never would have been in such a dark place without my dad."

"No," Jon cut me off, his voice firm. "When bad things happen, it shows who you really are. Your parents turned to drugs after your dad's injury. Eric tried to *murder* someone completely innocent. And you? All you've done is pour every bit of your energy into making yourself better. They had that chance, too, but they chose something different."

I swallowed. Was that true?

"You're a cycle breaker, Abi," he said. "The drugs, the violence, the abuse... it ended with you.

I'm the luckiest man alive to be with someone so kind and *good*. I can't believe I almost blew it."

Tears burned my eyes. I would never take Jon for granted again or think of him as anything other than a precious gift. I didn't deserve him; I had lucked out.

But maybe I *did* deserve something good after everything I'd been through. Maybe good things and bad things didn't happen for a reason. They just happened. And you had to take them as they came.

He pressed his lips to mine, and the tangy taste of salt blended with the sweet flavor of Jon. I held him close, savoring every second of our kiss. His lips were tender, soft, adoring. Our embrace was like falling into a hammock and rocking slowly, knowing everything, no matter what, would be okay, just because we had each other.

CHAPTER SIXTY-FOUR

WE LEFT AS SOON as we'd finished with the investigator. Jon drove the entire way to Woodman, holding my hand, but that still didn't feel close enough.

We didn't talk much, but his hand gripping mine said all there was to know. He had me. And he wasn't letting go.

Grandma called a couple of times on the way to check on me, but I couldn't bring myself to talk to her. Not yet. I just wanted to see her. To show her I was okay—or at least, going to be.

We arrived in Woodman late at night, after the stars were already twinkling in the sky and the moon hung like a silver orb straight above us. It seemed crazy they still shined after what happened.

Jon opened the door for me and walked me down the sidewalk to Grandma's house.

She didn't wait for us to get inside. The door flung open, and she raced toward us, tears already streaming down her lined face. She took me in the tightest hug I'd ever felt.

Jon hung on to my hand, but I hugged her back with everything I had left.

She pulled back, stroking my hair away from my face, touching my cheeks like she wanted to make sure I was real.

"Abi, you're okay. You're okay." She pulled me in again, sobbing against my shoulder. "I'm so glad you're okay."

"I had to be," I said, holding her tight. "I still have so much crap to give you about you *going steady* with Jorge."

She groaned and let out a half laugh, half sob. "Silly girl." But then she took my other hand and led us into the house. "Jon said you might be hungry, so I made everything."

Grandma's table practically sagged under plates and plates of food. Everything from dressing-less salad to grilled chicken and carrot sticks. But there was real food there too. Potato casseroles and a bowl of coleslaw that had to be more mayonnaise than cabbage.

I went straight for the serving spoon and ate a big bite, strips of cabbage hanging out of my mouth.

They both laughed, and Grandma said, "We got our girl back, didn't we?"

Jon grinned. "We sure did."

We ate to our hearts' content, until multiple plates had emptied and there was no more room in my stomach.

Grandma looked at me with love-filled eyes. "You need some rest."

I didn't want to go to bed after all that had happened, but I couldn't deny the bone-deep tiredness that touched every part of my body. Mostly, I didn't want to leave Jon.

She looked at him and said, "You're welcome to stay."

CHAPTER SIXTY-FIVE

JON and I crawled into my bed. Even though it was a queen and had so much more room than my bed in the dorm, we lay just as closely.

I faced him, letting my hand fall softly to his chest, right over his heart.

His fingers moved over my temple, brushing my hair back in a soothing pattern.

Our eyes held, admiring, marveling, savoring.

"I can't believe I almost lost you," he said.

"I don't want to think of that anymore," I replied, pushing up so I was over him, straddling him, my hair falling like a curtain around us. "I want to think of our future. One that never ends."

His eyes glittered as he nodded, understanding dawning on his face.

I dipped my head down and kissed him, slowly, like we had all the time in the world, but the truth was, we only had this night, this moment. That was all we were ever promised. I couldn't live another second not making the most of it.

With each slow kiss, each gentle touch, he cherished my body, adored it, until he traded spaces with me, hovering over me and pressing his weight against me as gently as he could. I gripped his shoulders and brought him closer to me for another kiss.

Breathing soft and slow, he feathered kisses along my cheek, along the bandages on my chin, down to my collarbone and the wrappings on my shoulder.

I reached down to peel off my shirt, struggled, but he helped me and then removed his own.

Our skin touched, warm, charged, safe. I wanted nothing to keep us apart, to stall this wonderful sensation spreading through my body. I made to pull up my sports bra, and he helped with that too, being gentle as it brushed against my bandages.

For a moment, he just stared, and I couldn't find it in me to be self-conscious. To worry about Denise and what she had or hadn't shared with him. I knew it would never come close to what I felt for him now. To what he so clearly felt for me.

We loved each other for the rest of the night until sweat slicked our foreheads and our bodies were spent. And then he held me close, his lips pressed against my forehead, as he whispered over and over again how much he loved me.

CHAPTER SIXTY-SIX

SOFT LIGHT SLANTED through my bedroom curtains, illuminating the smooth planes of Jon's face. I took him in, every inch, knowing he was completely and fully mine. Just like I was his. After last night, it could never be any other way.

I lay silently beside him until his eyelids fluttered to life, and he saw me through heavy lids, a smile slowly spreading across his face.

"Good morning, beautiful." His voice was husky. Perfect.

I smiled back at him. "Is this real life?"

He chuckled, pulling me closer to his chest. "How could it be anything else?"

Someone yelled from outside the room, and the door flew open. Stormy stood, wearing her apron from work, arms folded across her chest. "Abi almost gets murdered, and I have to hear about it on the *radio?*"

I shuffled back, pulling the blanket around my chest.

She rolled her eyes. "Oh, and you had sex. I suppose I was supposed to do my tarot cards to find that one out?"

"You don't do tarot cards," I said. "I think you're supposed to read them."

Her hands flew out at her sides, matching her exasperated expression. "That's not the point!" She hurried to me and held me close, wedging her arm between Jon and me. "Thank God you're okay."

I nodded. "I'm getting there."

She stepped back and caressed the not-yet-present bump of her stomach. "If I had to find another godmother for my baby, I would have found you in the afterlife and murdered you a second time."

I laughed. Harder than I should have.

She rolled her eyes, exasperated. "Get dressed, lovebirds, and meet me at the diner. I've got to get back to work." On the way out, she turned and held up a sticky note. "Oh, and your grandma's at some guy named Jorge's house. She'll be back at noon."

After the door shut behind her, Jon asked, "Are we going?"

"Yeah." I gave him a mischievous smile. "But there's something I want to do first."

I kissed him again, hungrier this time, playful, and we got lost in a tangle of sheets and limbs and *love*.

When it had been so long we were at risk of Stormy barging back in, we took separate showers and got dressed. The only clothes I had here were ones that were too big for me before I left for college.

None of them fit right, but I pulled on a pair of sweatpants with a drawstring and one of my many T-shirts. I stared at the words, tears forming in my eyes. *I love you from my head to-ma-toes.*

The restaurant was busy when we got there, but the second Stormy saw us, she turned over her shoulder and yelled into the kitchen window, "I'm taking fifteen!"

Jon held my hand and led me to an open booth, the farthest one from anyone else, and sat down on the same side as me. I loved the way his arm snaked around my shoulders and rested there, like that was where it belonged. Where I belonged.

Stormy came over and flopped down into the booth, causing the cushion to let out a whoosh of air.

She ignored it and put her elbows on the table. "Tell me everything."

I told the story, and the more I said it out loud, the more I realized the depth of horror that had happened to me. I had been through hell and back twice now. But I had survived each time.

When I finished, there were tears in her eyes that she wiped away. "If he doesn't die, I'll go murder him myself."

I shook my head. I didn't know what to hope for. Wishing him dead would make me too similar to him. But having him alive meant knowing there was someone on the planet who wanted, and attempted, to have me dead.

"What are you doing next?" she asked. "Are you going back to college?"

I sighed. "I don't even know if they'll take me back. I broke the nutritionist's rules on day one."

Jon gently rubbed my back. "We'll figure it out. And if not, we'll transfer somewhere cheaper next year."

My mouth fell open at what that meant. "You'd do that?" He'd be giving up everything for me.

"I'd do anything to be where you are."

Stormy pretended to gag herself.

Someone yelled her name from the kitchen, and she rolled her eyes.

"I'm going back to work," she said. Then she reached out and lifted my chin, holding her fingers beneath it so I had to look at her.

"I love you, *chica*. I would kill for you." Then she looked at Jon. "Don't you ever forget that."

CHAPTER SIXTY-SEVEN

MR. SCOLLER CALLED the college and pulled some strings that may have included a few legal threats.

Jon and I would go back on Tuesday, my nineteenth birthday, our athletic scholarships intact. All homework waived. It was the best present I could have asked for.

Jon might have argued that he had given me a better package.

I might have hit him.

But I did have to meet with the nutritionist and follow through on her rules. I wasn't crazy about the hours it would take out of my week, but I would do it. Even though I wanted to live in the moment, I had to remember there was an endgame bigger than my twelve by twelve dorm. I had a future to think about. One that included Jon and hopefully a family.

Before we left though, Grandma wanted to take me to lunch, just the two of us.

I agreed, trying not to show her just how much I wanted to stay. I loved being in Woodman, being home with my grandma. At least here I wasn't a ship in the middle of the ocean, floating in the dark and searching for land.

Plus, I never had to worry about being anyone but myself around Grandma or our friends. They accepted me as I was, knowing my past, my flaws, how I used to look. This was home. But to be able to come back, I needed to leave.

Grandma and I went to the same restaurant where Jon took me to breakfast the first time. Where our families sat together and shared a meal. Where Jon told me that attractive guys—like him—would ask me out, go on dates with me, if they just took the time to know me.

My insides warmed. Jon had *chosen* me. He *knew* me. I would remember that always.

"You sure are thinking about something," Grandma said behind her menu.

I looked up at her. "What?"

"You haven't said a word since we left the

house," she commented. "Are you worried about that scumbag? You know, even if he gets out of the hospital, he will never have access to you again. I will make sure of it. You hear me?"

"Whoa, whoa, whoa, Grandma," I said, half admiring of her steely gaze and half intimidated. "I know. It's not that."

She set her menu down and looked at me, worry in her eyes. "What is it then?"

"How are things ever supposed to go back to normal?"

Grandma's mouth set in a determined line. "Listen to me, okay? If you hear anything I say, I want it to be this."

I nodded, waited.

"Once there was a man who fell into the subway in New York City. He got caught between the train and the wall. When the firefighters got there, they realized that the train had cut through his internal organs. The thing that had injured him was the only thing keeping him alive. They knew the second they moved the train, he would die.

"When you grow up in a home like yours, where your parents are always fighting or you're getting beaten down every single day, you start to feel like that guy trapped in the subway. You hate the train that's keeping you there, but you don't know how to live without it.

"And when that train moves, you panic. You search for anything that resembles that train to keep you together because you don't know how to exist out of that chaos. And if you can't find anything wrong, you create it. In school, in your eating habits, and in your relationships. Do you understand?"

I shifted in my seat, feeling the uncomfortable truth of her words work through me.

"You haven't gotten used to living outside of chaos yet, Abi. But it's your choice. Are you going to find another train, or are you going to learn to live without it?"

CHAPTER 68

That's how I found myself in the nutritionist's office, ready to eat a truckload of crow, along with whatever else she asked of me. Even if it included red meat and ranch dressing.

I was worth it. My future was worth it.

She stared across her fake wood desk at me and said, "It's good to see you, Abi."

I nodded, cringing. "Are you ready to tell me you told me so?"

A sad look crossed her face, and she shook her head. "I spoke to the counselor you'll be working with on campus, and she said a lot of times eating disorders are about control. The worst thing I could have done for you was tell you everything to eat and make someone watch."

I mean, she wasn't wrong.

"So." She lifted a packet of paper and threw it in the trash. Then she pulled a new packet of paper out of her drawer and handed it to me. "These are healthy eating guidelines and calorie goals for you based on your current weight, height, and activity level. You have the power to make yourself strong instead of skinny. Powerful instead of weak. The choice is yours."

"I choose strong," I replied, even though I didn't need to. "But..." I pointed at her trash can. "Did you plan that beforehand?"

Her cheeks flushed. "I might have wanted to make an impact."

I laughed. "You definitely did."

She stood and extended her hand. "So, allies?"

Her grip felt tight in mine, and I squeezed it back. "Teammates."

I left the office with the packet tucked under my arm and just enjoyed the cool fall air. I had something to look forward to as well: the fact that I was walking back to my dorm to meet Jon, who would take me out to lunch since we were both done with our classes and practice for the day.

We could just enjoy the day together. We needed that.

But then I opened the door to my dorm with the loudest chorus of "SURPRISE!" I'd ever heard.

I never knew this many people could fit in a dorm room, but here they were. All of my friends from Woodman. My grandma. Jorge Cordes. Marta and Glen. My new friends, Nikki, Mollie, Jayne. Anika. And my forever. Jon.

There was a stack of presents on my desk, but I couldn't care less. I was just excited to see my friends!

The Woodman crew caught me first, one after another wrapping me in a tight hug. Roberto, Andrew, and Skye couldn't make it, but I would see them over Thanksgiving break. I couldn't wait.

And when I cycled through them, I came face to face with Nikki. She jutted out her chin like she was ready for an attack, but instead I pulled her into a tight hug and said, "Thank you for looking out for me. You're an amazing friend."

Her muscles relaxed, and she hugged me back. "Don't scare me like that again!" Then she pulled back. "But Eric? I never thought he would do anything to hurt you."

"I don't want to talk about him," I said, looking around the room. "We have way better people to be thinking about."

She nodded. "You're right."

I smiled. "Let me introduce you to my friends."

My Woodman friends greeted her and the other girls like they were long-lost best friends. Just like on my first day of school at Woodman, Stormy made sure they were being included in the conversation, along with Anika.

My circle was growing, along with my heart.

Then Marta and Glen approached me, Glen holding a small card wrapped in a ribbon.

Marta took me into another hug that made me so happy her son was the one I fell in love with.

Then Glen gave me a side-armed hug and held out the card. I looked up at him and saw him incline his head toward Grandma and Jorge.

As they walked over, I pulled away the ribbon and peeled open the envelope.

Inside was a postcard showing a small resort town. Red River. On the reverse side, it had a happy birthday note from Glen and Marta.

I looked up at them, waiting for an explanation, and Grandma said, "We're going on the Christmas trip with them this year!"

"Our treat," Marta said. "It's time the whole family came."

I grinned and thanked them to no end. I couldn't wait to make memories with them in the mountains. Maybe even try skiing or snowboarding for the first time.

After a few hours, the party died down until Jon and I were the last ones in the dorm room.

I stared around us, at the remnants of something amazing. And then it hit me. All this time, I'd hoped I had gold filling my cracks and holding me together. Why hadn't I seen that my gold was all around me? My friends and family coming together to love me, no matter what, holding me up when I couldn't even support myself.

There had been gold there all along. The biggest piece stood only feet away from me, smiling down at me like I was the greatest treasure of all.

"What now, birthday girl?" he asked.

I smiled up at him. "I want to unwrap my present."

"Of course." He started toward my desk and the gifts that rested on it, but I tugged at his shirt, going the opposite direction.

"I meant you."

***

Thank you for reading *Abi and the Boy Who Lied*!
Continue reading for a free preview into the final book in Abi's story, *Abi and the Boy She Loves*.

Use this QR code to discover the final
book in Abi's story!

ABI AND THE BOY SHE LOVES: FREE PREVIEW

This was exactly where Jon belonged. On the track, the wind he created flying through his hair, his face determined, his lungs heaving, his muscles rippling with every labored step.

My cheers for him blended with his parents', Grandma's, Jorge's, and everyone else there to support the runners at the first indoor meet of the season. Each lap they made with Jon edging steadily ahead only reinforced how invested he was in this sport. How right the coaches had been to recruit him.

The closer he and his competitors got to the end, the louder the entire place grew until all I could hear was an echoing of yells and claps. I watched his feet, barely touching the ground before lifting and pressing forward. Ahead.

He crossed the finish line at the front of the pack. His steps slowed, but his chest lifted and fell rapidly. He laced his fingers behind his head and sucked in big gasps for air. As sweat slicked his skin, I thought he had never looked more beautiful.

Not like the photo Marta snapped of me after my race. My skin was ruddy, and my frizzy hair was desperately attempting to escape my ponytail. It wasn't fair. But then again, I didn't have to look at myself until I'd had a good shower. I could keep taking in the sight of Jon all day long, though.

I probably should put my tongue back in my mouth before someone slipped on my drool and got hurt. But still. Damn.

I absently scratched at my shoulder, then stopped myself. My skin was healing, which only meant the scabs itched like crazy. Especially with the dried sweat irritating it. I was so ready for a good shower and a dinner out with our families.

I waited in the stands with them while the awards ceremony took place. I hadn't won any of my events, but I hadn't placed last either. For me, that was the same as winning, and for the first meet of the season, I was thankful to just be...average. For once. It meant I belonged here too. I wasn't just a charity case anymore; I was a part of the team.

But Jon stood out on the platform as they placed a medal around his neck. The corners of his lips tugged against a smile as he tried acting like he wasn't over-the-moon excited about his win.

When we finished clapping and cheering, I leaned over to the others and said, "I'm going to the team meeting, and then I'll take a quick shower."

Marta smiled at me. "Take your time, sweetie. Our dinner reservation isn't 'til six."

The watch on my wrist said we were still an hour and a half off, which royally stunk. I was starving.

Turned out, a girl could get used to eating more. And still do well in college track.

Grandma stood up and gave me a tight squeeze.

"I'm going to get you all sweaty!" I cried.

She held on even tighter. "It's worth it. I'm so proud of you."

I hugged her back and said, "Thank you," even though the words didn't convey enough. I wouldn't be here without her.

I went down to the place where the girls' distance team was supposed to meet and sat on the floor beside Nikki. She was absently stretching, not really putting too much effort into it.

"You did awesome today," I said.

She smiled. "It wasn't first."

"It wasn't last either," I said. "Second place isn't anything to turn your nose up at."

She pushed the end of her nose up and snorted like a pig.

I shoved her shoulder, laughing.

"Okay, ladies," Coach Cadence said, silencing us and our teammates. "We had a good first meet today. We placed sixth as a team, which is very promising for our season."

We let out a few exhausted whoops, and she smiled until we quieted down.

She went around the group, offering congratulations and quick pieces of advice, but she skipped me.

"Go shower up," she said. And then she added, "Abi, can you stay behind?"

I nodded, not wanting to meet her eyes. I'd been happy with how I ran, but now I wondered if I should be worried. Had I done something wrong?

As the other girls left, I stood up to face whatever Coach Cadence had to say to me.

"How are you doing?" she asked.

"Good?" I eyed her, waiting for the real reason she asked me to stay behind.

Her chocolate eyes were softer now. "I know you've had a hard start to your semester, but I'm proud of how far you've come, and you should be too."

Relief flooded my chest, making my heart buoy so high I worried it might float away. My lightweight sneakers wouldn't do anything to keep the rest of me on the ground. "You mean it?"

With a smile, she nodded. "You've worked hard to get better, both on the track and up here." She tapped her forehead.

I just nodded because weekly therapy sessions hadn't been easy. My therapist dug through the darkest corners of my mind—of my past—and worked with all the painful memories until I was exhausted in every sense of the word. It was all I could do to go back to my dorm and curl up for a nap afterwards.

"Now, go shower up." She nodded toward the stands where I'd been sitting with Jon's parents, Grandma, and Jorge. "It looks like you've got some fans waiting to celebrate you."

"Thanks, Coach," I said.

My smile was still on my face as I showered, changed, and met the others in the stands. Jon was nowhere to be seen, so I guessed he was still getting cleaned up.

Grandma gripped my arm. "Can you show me where the bathroom is?"

"Sure." We walked through the thinning crowd to a bathroom. I stood off to the side to wait for Grandma, but she stopped beside me.

"We need to talk."

I girded my heart as I stepped closer to the cinderblock wall, away from the other people walking by. "What's going on? Are you okay?"

My mind was going to all the horrible places. Cancer. Disease. Financial struggles. I needed her to just tell me so I could quit imagining every terrible scenario.

"Your father is up for parole."

Continue reading Abi and the Boy She Loves today!

Use this QR code to discover the final book in Abi's story!

ALSO BY KELSIE STELTING

The Curvy Girl Club

Curvy Girls Can't Date Quarterbacks

Curvy Girls Can't Date Billionaires

Curvy Girls Can't Date Cowboys

Curvy Girls Can't Date Bad Boys

Curvy Girls Can't Date Best Friends

Curvy Girls Can't Date Bullies

Curvy Girls Can't Dance

Curvy Girls Can't Date Soldiers

Curvy Girls Can't Date Princes

The Texas High Series

Chasing Skye: Book One

Becoming Skye: Book Two

Loving Skye: Book Three

Anika Writes Her Soldier

Abi and the Boy Next Door: Book One

Abi and the Boy Who Lied: Book Two

Abi and the Boy She Loves: Book Three

The Pen Pal Romance Series

Dear Adam

Fabio Vs. the Friend Zone

Sincerely Cinderella

The Sweet Water High Series: A Multi-Author Collaboration

Road Trip with the Enemy: A Sweet Standalone Romance

YA Contemporary Romance Anthology

The Art of Taking Chances

Nonfiction

Raising the West

Sometimes healing means admitting we still have more work to do. It is unbelievably easy to fall into the trap of thinking we've done the work, we've moved on. Case closed. Problem solved.

But real life isn't like that. We can go to weekly therapy for three years, take a year off, get triggered, and need to go right back. We can train up a weak ankle, catch it on a rock, and be at square one all over again. Like Abi, we can get the guy, have great friends, live with a loving adult, and still have trouble loving ourselves.

As a romance writer, I know how easy it is to tie up a story in a nice little happily-ever-after bow. While I sincerely believe in happy endings and finding healing, I had to be honest in this second book. Having Abi and Jon realize they were made for each other wouldn't fix the years of trauma Abi experienced at the hands of her parents and peers. It would only provide Abi a safe and loving person to be with her as she navigated her new life.

Let's stop looking at healing and happily ever after's as finite endings that prevent all future struggles. Let's remember that they give us something beautiful to hold on to when life has us down. Just because Abi backslid, she shouldn't have felt hopeless. She should have felt human. We all have those days where we go one step forward and two steps back. But we also have days that move us miles forward. We can't forget that each step, even the small ones, even the hard ones, matter. They build up our strength so over time we can look back and see just how far we've come.

ACKNOWLEDGMENTS

When the first reader emailed me about writing a second book in Abi's story, I was flattered. When a few more asked for the same thing, I realized I needed to give it some real thought. And then I realized I had some fears to overcome. Mostly, would my second book live up to the first?

I want to thank each and every one of my readers who pushed for a second book. Without you, I wouldn't have found the joy I felt in living in Abi's world a little while longer. I wouldn't have pushed myself this hard to give a satisfying story. I wouldn't be writing these acknowledgments right now!

I also have to thank an author friend, Anne-Marie Meyer for encouraging me to continue the series. She gave me a much-needed push and some extra confidence I needed. Another friend, Sally Henson, spoke with me throughout the journey, cheering me on and helping to calm my fears.

Also, some real appreciation should be given to my mom, who almost every time I talked to her on the phone asked me where I was at on Abi's second story and reminded me that I should be writing!

My husband and children supported me by giving me time to write, which always seems to be in short supply these days! Luckily, my husband makes weekend mornings away from mom fun instead of tragic so I can write guilt-free and without worrying the house will fall apart in my absence.

When I wrote this book, I knew I was sending it to good hands! My editor, Tricia Harden, has an amazing talent to shape and care for words while honoring the author's voice, and working with her is always a joy.

I always want you, the reader, to know how absolutely valued and appreciated you are. When you picked up this story, you offered your time, your mind, your heart to these words. I am honored you chose to spend time with my characters and I hope it was worth every second. Thank you for being the best part of my writing.

ABOUT THE AUTHOR

Kelsie Stelting is a body positive romance author who writes love stories with strong characters, deep feelings, and happy endings.

She currently lives in Colorado. You can often find her writing, spending time with family, and soaking up too much sun wherever she can find it.

Visit www.kelsiestelting.com to get a

free story and sign up for her readers' group!

 facebook.com/kelsiesteltingcreative

 twitter.com/kelsiestelting

 instagram.com/kelsiestelting

Made in the USA
Monee, IL
22 October 2021